KIDCO STRIKES BACK!

"What do you think we should do, Dickie?" Bette asked.

"I don't know!" Dickie cried out, looking up with teary eyes at his sisters, a broken boy. "The whole thing's falling apart! The government's after us . . . we can't make any money anymore . . . You were right a long time ago, Bette. Childish, two-bit stunts! That's all Kidco is."

The three girls looked at one another, not sure what to do. Bette finally rose and walked over to her brother, telling him softly, "Dickie, I said that about all the other stuff, you did. Not Kidco. Kidco's the best thing I've ever been a part of."

"But Kidco's kaput," he sniffed.

"No way, Dickie," Bette said. "I'm not giving up!"

"Me neither!" said June.

"Me either, too!" NeNe chipped in.

Finally Dickie said, "You're right! Who do they think they're pushing around?"

"That's the spirit!" Bette said.

"So, are we gonna stick together and fight?" Dickie asked.

"Of course!" June said.

"With our last ounce of manure!" Bette promised.

TWENTIETH CENTURY-FOX

Presents

A FRANK YABLANS Presentation

A RONALD F. MAXWELL Film

KIDCO

SCOTT SCHWARTZ
CLIFTON JAMES

Music by Michael Small

Written by BENNETT TRAMER

Produced by FRANK YABLANS and DAVID NIVEN JR.

Directed by RONALD F. MAXWELL

KIDCO

Ron Renauld

Based on the screenplay by
Bennett Tramer

BANTAM BOOKS
TORONTO · NEW YORK · LONDON · SYDNEY

KIDCO
A Bantam Book / November 1983

ISBN 0-553-23787-X

Published simultaneously in the United States and Canada

Bantam Books are published by Bantam Books, Inc. Its trademark, consisting of the words "Bantam Books" and the portrayal of a rooster, is Registered in U.S. Patent and Trademark Office and in other countries. Marca Registrada. Bantam Books, Inc., 666 Fifth Avenue, New York, New York 10103.

PRINTED IN THE UNITED STATES OF AMERICA

H 0 9 8 7 6 5 4 3 2 1

For Bob, Trix, Marie, Dave,
Laura and Linda—enterprising
brothers and sisters all.

Thanks to Ms. Miller-Renauld
and to Mr. Persistence, Jon Brown.

THIS STORY IS BASED ON TRUE INCIDENTS . . .

. . . NO KIDDING!

Prologue

A sprawl of mammoth boulders blemished the face of the Cuyamaca Mountains like rampant warts of stone, but winter rains had coaxed forth enough greenery to help soften the rugged harshness of the steep terrain. Manzanita and the thick, waxy leaves of great oaks stirred heartily in the breeze, and wild grass clung in tenacious pockets wherever it had been able to throw down roots, providing a vibrant backdrop for the rest of the chaparral. Birds flitted through the brush, and a pair of long-limbed rabbits scrambled speedily across the winding band of asphalt that carved its way from the mountaintops to the rolling valley below. A lone black sedan negotiated the turns with gear-grinding timidity, while inside the car two men stared out the windshield, one keeping his eyes on the road while the other let his gaze wander over the scenery.

"Hey, get a load of that sign," the passenger said, pointing to the side of the road.

"No way," the driver said, downshifting as he went into a wide turn. "I've got my hands full keeping this tank on the road. I've been on amusement rides tamer than this."

"'Welcome to Ramona, California. Population, 15,201'," the passenger read aloud as they passed the sign. "'Former Turkey Capital of the World.' Some claim to fame, huh?"

Reaching a length of straightaway, the driver glanced at his younger partner and smirked, "I hear they named your hometown the new turkey capital in your honor, Porzinski."

"Oh, aren't you the funny one, Sloman," Porzinksi deadpanned, adjusting his silk tie and straightening the lapels of his navy blue suitcoat. In his late thirties, Porzinski had a bulging forehead and large, droopy eyes that had a fixed glaze of ruthless intensity. Stubbing out a cigarette in the dashboard ashtray, he grumbled, "Just what the government needs is more comedians on its payroll."

"Hey, lighten up, Phil," Sloman said as he negotiated the last few turns before the road leveled out toward the small town that filled the valley floor. "No reason why we can't enjoy ourselves. Hell, with a job like this, a guy needs all the humor he can manage, right?"

"Is that why you wear that clown suit?" Porzinski said, eyeing his partner's loud, checkered blazer and clashing tie. Mel Sloman was as short and squat as Porzinski was tall and lean. It was no wonder that they were known around the office as Abbott and Costello.

"Listen, Phil, if you want to look like you just left a funeral, that's your problem," Sloman said with a smile, rolling down his window to let out the stale smoke from Porzinski's cigarette. "Me, I want to look like a man who knows how to enjoy the better things in life."

"Polyester is one of the better things in life?" Porzinski wondered aloud as he reached for another cigarette. Lighting it, he blinked through the rising smoke at the surrounding farmland that marked the outskirts of Ramona. "I hope we can find this Cessna guy right off and wrap things up quick. I hate small towns."

"Why's that?"

"People are too damn uppity, that's why. They all have such a narrow view of things, they think they have all the answers." Porzinski rolled down his own window and blew smoke out into the clear day. "What do you want to bet we get the royal runaround once we track Cessna down?"

"How about lunch?"

"You're on," Porzinski said.

Lapsing into silence, the men started looking for the address listed on Porzinski's clipboard as the black sedan swooped into town like a four-wheeled vulture seeking its prey.

One

If Norman Rockwell were alive and under doctor's orders to live someplace where the weather was benevolent and the pace of life slow, he might have chosen Ramona, which looked as if its town planners had taken their cues from Rockwell's covers for the *Saturday Evening Post*. Buffered by the formidable Cuyamacas against too many intrusions from the outside world, Ramona reeked of all that small towns are noted for. It also reeked of the pungent odors that came with the farming industry that was the backbone of much of the community. A ride down the town's only main street revealed shopfronts with signs that told almost all one needed to know about the makeup of its population. The Four-H Club, the Future Farmers of America, the Kiwanis Club, the Rotary Club, the American Legion, Faith Tabernacle. These were people steeped in old values, content to live lives of hard work and modest aspiration.

Then there was Dickie Cessna.

In the dingy shadows of the Ramona Day School maintenance room, the thirteen-year-old was in the midst of his most recent scheme for making money. Standing in front of the janitor's bench, he carefully screwed in the nozzle of an industrial vacuum cleaner into the side opening he'd made in a five gallon plastic bottle that had once carried purified water. It now held Ping-Pong balls, dozens of them, each one numbered on the side with a marking pen. As a handful of his fellow students watched anxiously, Dickie leaned over and flicked the vacuum on. The motor had been rigged so that it expelled air rather than drawing it in, and Dickie's freckled face lit up triumphantly as the Ping-Pong balls began to bound crazily off the sides of the plastic container, making a sound like amplified popcorn. One of the balls finally found its way out of the mouth of the bottle and into Dickie's waiting hand.

"Number twenty-one," he called out to his sister, NeNe, a ponytailed nine-year-old who tallied the number on a nearby chalkboard. Across the room, one student yipped with excitement as the others groaned.

"Number seven," Dickie said, withdrawing the second ball to make its escape from the bottle. A steady stream of the numbered orbs followed, and NeNe screeched the chalk across the board in her haste to keep up with her brother.

"Number thirty-two . . . number eight . . . number fifteen . . ."

Standing between Dickie and NeNe was Skip Russo, Dickie's closest friend and the afternoon's sergeant-at-arms. Although he wasn't quite as tall as Dickie, he was solidly built, and watched the other students with a foreboding gaze he'd practiced regularly since seeing his first Clint Eastwood movie. His arms were crossed and his pudgy jaw was clenched. A toothpick rolled back and forth between his tightened lips like a rifle poking out of a prison guard tower.

"Number forty-one . . . and number twelve," Dickie concluded, setting aside the last ball and quickly turning off the vacuum before another one could worm its way to freedom. "That's our fifteen lucky numbers. Winners, please bring up your cards. Losers, there'll be another game in a minute. . . ."

Sitting down in an old swivel chair the janitor hadn't gotten around to fixing yet, Dickie set a shining coin changer on his lap and grabbed the carbon copies of the cards carried by the students who were lining up before him. He took the card from a diminutive eighth grader, flashing her a professional smile before checking her marks on the card against the copy and the numbers NeNe had posted on the board.

"Eight out of fifteen pays two-to-one, on a quarter . . ." Dickie clicked the coin changer and handed the girl her winnings. "Congratulations, Louise. Next?"

As another of Dickie's classmates stepped up and thrust his card out for inspection, Dickie glanced over at his sister, who was standing idly in front of the board, wiping the chalk off her fingers as she watched the payoffs.

"NeNe!" Dickie chided impatiently. "The drinks!"

With a sigh, NeNe moved over and picked up a small Styrofoam cooler from the bench and carried it over to the other students, barking out like a seasoned carney, "Coke, Pepsi, Mountain Dew, Seven-Up. Forty-five cents a can!"

Louise was in the process of trading her winnings for a chilled Tab when the sound of a key slipping into a lock turned a dozen heads toward the door. Louise almost dropped her drink, and a few of the other students let out involuntary gasps as the door suddenly swung inward. A huge, burly man lumbered into the room, wearing a thick beard and a janitor's uniform in need of a good washing. He looked over the students with deep, brooding eyes, then turned to Dickie and said, "I got the money from the second grade."

"Good work, Charlie," Dickie said as the janitor came over, pulling several folded keno cards and a handful of change from his pockets. Forsaking the other students for the moment, Dickie took the cards and money from Charlie and shook his head with disappointment as he scrutinized it. "A nickel bet . . . four cents?! Sheesh, with the measly allowance these kids get, it's hardly worth the trouble." Glancing up at Charlie, he asked, "Where's the twenty cents Tommy Perkins owes us?"

"He doesn't have it yet," Charlie explained. "Says his parents'll pay him next time he loses a tooth."

Skip Russo stepped forward, pushing up the sleeves of his oversized football jersey and speaking in a voice that was midway through puberty, threatening to crack any second as he tried to sound like someone three times his age. "Want me to help him lose it?"

"Nah," Dickie said, setting the keno cards aside and feeding the money into his coin changer. "Save the rough stuff for fifty cents and up."

Disappointed, Skip backed up to the blackboard and let his sleeves down. As Charlie moved away to load up his broom cart for postschool sweeping, Dickie turned his attention back to matters at hand.

"Next!"

Harvey Peterjohn, a thin, well-dressed boy a few months shy of his thirteenth birthday, took a step forward and sneered at Dickie as he tossed his card on the desk. "Eight winners," he boasted snidely. "On a dollar!"

"Hang on, Harvey," Dickie said, looking away from the opened palm thrust out in front of his face. "Let me check my copy. . . ."

"Hey, I don't have all day, you know," Harvey complained, shifting on his feet and hitching his pants up.

After comparing cards, Dickie glanced up and said, "You only marked *seven*, Harvey."

"What're you trying to pull?!" Harvey whined indignantly, almost before Dickie had a chance to finish talking. He leaned over and jabbed a skinny forefinger at his card, protesting, "See!? Number forty-one's marked on my card. I just didn't press hard enough for it to show up on your copy, that's all. Now pay up!"

Dickie waited calmly for Harvey to play out his performance, then he flicked the quarter switch on his coin changer four times and handed the money to him, saying, "I run a clean game, Harvey. Take your dollar back . . . and leave."

Harvey ignored the quarters and put his hands on his hips, raising his strident voice another octave. "Look, Cessna, you can't throw me out of here just because I . . ."

Skip vaulted forward, glad for the chance to put on a show of his own. Wedging himself between Dickie and Harvey, he rose on his tiptoes as he started fumbling with the sleeves of his jersey again. "Beat it," he told Harvey with calculated menace.

Harvey's arms dropped to his side and his fury seemed to be draining out from the soles of his penny loafers. Avoiding Skip's icy gaze, he reached around and plucked the quarters from Dickie's hand, then pivoted about and rushed past Charlie, leaving the room.

"That's telling him, Skip!" NeNe said, beaming at her brother's friend.

"He's nothing but a spoiled brat," Louise added. "Good riddance to him, I say."

"I saw the creep cheating on his card," another student claimed.

"Hey, we didn't need his cooties anyway," Dickie said, trying to restore order as quickly as possible. Time was money. "NeNe, pass out cards for the next game."

"Anybody else want a drink first?" NeNe asked the others.

"You got a root beer?" Charlie asked, looking up from his brooms.

"Nice and cold," NeNe said cheerfully, going over to the

janitor and pulling a can from the cooler. "Only forty-five cents."

"What do you mean, *only*?" Charlie complained good-naturedly as he sorted through his change for a pair of quarters. "I can get the same thing from a vending machine for thirty cents."

"Yes, but you won't get service with a smile," Dickie told him from across the room. "Listen, Charlie, do you think you can get bets from the fourth grade, too?"

"Sure," the janitor said, popping open his root beer and swilling down a quick few swallows. "I'll tell Mrs. Cooper I gotta check the radiator."

As Charlie left the room and closed the door behind him, Dickie quickly paid off the other winners, then began stuffing the stray Ping-Pong balls back into the makeshift hopper. NeNe passed out cards and began collecting bets as Dickie launched into his well-practiced spiel.

"All right, it's keno time again. Pick your numbers, everybody. Sixty balls in the air, and I grab the first fifteen to pop out of the bottle. Eight out of fifteen pays two-to-one on the quarter; nine out of fifteen, three-to-one; ten out of fifteen, four-to-one and so forth. . . ."

The door swung open once more, this time admitting a dour-faced middle-aged man in a dark suit, wearing a bow tie and a look of harassment pushed to the limit.

"Mr. Ruggles!!" NeNe gasped with horror, voicing the sentiments of the other children in the room. Mr. Ruggles was the principal of Ramona Day School.

"So . . ." Mr. Ruggles said, bobbing his head with deprecation at the youthful throng. "*This* is where the eighth grade spends its recess!"

"You can skin your knees on the blacktop," Dickie offered lamely.

"Shut up, Richard, and come with me!" Mr. Ruggles commanded, pointing one finger out the door. Looking at NeNe, he added, "You, too, Jeannine! Everybody else, out!"

Fueled by fear, the students streamed past Mr. Ruggles and out into the hallway. Even Skip was unable to keep up his dauntless facade. He smiled gamely at the principal on his way out the door, almost tripping over Charlie's broom cart. The jolt was enough to snap him out of his fright, and he slowly lapsed back into character as he followed Mr. Ruggles and the two Cessna children out of the maintenance room.

Harvey Peterjohn was leaning over the water cooler just down the corridor, and he pulled his head away in time to grin mockingly at Dickie and flip him a one-finger salute.

"You snitch!" Dickie shouted.

Skip took the accusation as his signal to go to work, and he started down the hall for Harvey.

"Skip!" Mr. Ruggles called out.

When Skip failed to heed the principal and continued to advance, Harvey backed into the wall, shrieking with panic, "I'll tell my father!"

"Yeah, well, you'll sound pretty funny talking to him with no teeth, Peterjohn!" Skip railed.

Before Skip could make good on his threat, though, Dickie caught up with him and placed a restraining hand on his shoulder. "Forget it, Skip. The house was losing today, anyway."

Skip reluctantly unflexed his fists and glowered a few seconds at Harvey before skulking off to his locker. Mr. Ruggles could only shake his head with resignation at the boys, wondering how many more days like this he would have to suffer through before his pension was ensured. Leading Dickie and NeNe away from the others, he lapsed into a weary lecture, one that he'd obviously given before.

"I just don't understand you, Dickie. Why don't you apply your leadership potential, and all the energy you devote to running these scams, to legitimate school activities?"

"They don't pay as well," Dickie replied nonchalantly. As they rounded the corner, he looked up at Mr. Ruggles and asked, "So, what's it gonna be? No trips to the zoo? A note from our parents?"

Reaching his office, Mr. Ruggles opened the door and gestured for the children to go inside. With chilling firmness, he said, "No Richard, I think we're past that stage."

Two

"Suspended?!"

NeNe mouthed the word as if it were a death sentence Principal Ruggles had levied against her and Dickie. It had been over half an hour ago, but his stern voice was still ringing in her ears as she and her brother pedaled their Stingray bicycles along a stretch of newly paved roadway leading to one of the first signs that the present was at long last encroaching upon Ramona. Specifically, the sign read:

WELCOME TO
SAN DIEGO COUNTRY ESTATES
A PLANNED RESORT COMMUNITY

From the looks of the widespread construction taking place, Ramona would soon be doubling its population. Condominiums, villas and ranch houses were sprouting like fungus after a hard rain, and work crews were laying sewer lines along the streets that would connect all the new homes to the main road that ran through the Ramona of old.

"Suspended!" NeNe wailed miserably once more as they made their way up the slight grade past a mud-caked earthmover the size of a dinosaur.

"Hey, Ruggles did us a favor," Dickie panted philosophically, leaning over his handlebars to get more power out of his pedaling. "All they teach us is a bunch of junk we could never use in business. I mean, who cares what the capital of South Dakota is?"

All along the road, plastic flags snapped in the wind, and there was a wide, red banner stretched between two newly planted trees proclaiming GRAND OPENING! The sound of hammers and power saws filled the air, drowning out the bleat of cattle in the distant fields. The children were oblivious to all this activity, however, and NeNe was still entrenched in her melancholy.

"We always get caught," she puffed, trying to keep up with her brother.

"Don't start that, NeNe," Dickie said.

"We always get caught," NeNe repeated, jutting out her lower lip petulantly.

Just past the new housing development was a rambling golf course, lush with green grass and swollen with countless knolls and hillocks. Dickie slowed down, watching the groundskeeping crew engaging in their daily rituals of grooming the course.

"Look, this time it's just as well," he told his sister. "Charlie was charging us eight bucks an hour for the maintenance room, and all those second and third graders were bad credit risks. We have bigger things in store for us, and I bet they're right around here!"

Dickie pulled his bike off the street and onto the thick grass of the parkway. As he gazed reflectively at the course and its surrounding guest lodge, tennis courts, swimming pools, and fairway condominiums, NeNe reluctantly pulled to a stop next to him, complaining, "Come on, Dickie! You *always* stop here. . . ."

"Will ya look at all this, NeNe?" Dickie said excitedly, gesturing with a sweep of his hand at the latest additions to the outskirts of Ramona.

"It looks the same way it did yesterday," NeNe griped, squinting her eyes against the slanting rays of the afternoon sun. "Except they put more traps in the gopher holes. . . ."

"Oh, NeNe you're looking at it all wrong. . . ."

"What am I supposed to do, look cross-eyed or something?"

"Don't you see what this means—a resort right here in Ramona? It means people'll be coming here from all over California. . . from all over the country. . . from Tibet, probably!" Swept up by his vision, his voice took on an increasingly dramatic tone. "It's a gold mine, NeNe! Right in our own back yard. You and me have been hustling for nickels and dimes long enough. This is our chance to start making the big bucks!"

"No way, Jose," NeNe groused. "I'm retiring."

"What did you say?" Dickie exclaimed, staring at his sister in disbelief.

"I said I'm retiring," NeNe insisted. "From now on I'm only selling cookies for the Campfire Girls."

Dickie inched his bike over until their front tires touched, then leaned forward so that he faced NeNe eye-to-eye. "Is that what you want out of life? Cookies? A lemonade stand? A lousy paper route? Is that all it takes to—"

"It is for now! I'm only in the fourth grade, Dickie!"

Dickie rolled his eyes with disgust and sat back on his bike, shaking his head. "So, you'll waste your time goofing around on the playground, and you know what? Before you know it, NeNe, you'll be in high school! Then all you can do is get good grades so you can get into college. Then you gotta get good grades in college so you can get a job! And then you wind up working for someone else, making *them* money . . . or, in your case, maybe you'll end up depending on your *husband's* crummy job to pay the bills while you're raising a bunch of kids!" With a knowing snicker, Dickie bored his gaze into NeNe and continued, " 'Only in the fourth grade' . . . You better wise up before it's too late!"

"Too late? Dickie, I'm three years and two weeks away from my first period!"

"That's no excuse!" Dickie blurted defiantly. "This is a land of great opportunity . . . for kids, too! You think the Declaration of Independence says 'Life, liberty and the pursuit of happiness, but first you gotta show your I.D.'?"

"I don't know," NeNe confessed. "We don't study the Declaration of Independence till next semester . . . if they let me back in."

NeNe turned her bike around and pedaled back onto the road. Dickie followed alongside her, taunting, "Okay, *be* a housewife. Just don't say I didn't warn you. . . ."

As Dickie pulled ahead of her, NeNe stuck her tongue out at him. They rode on in single file, heading away from the new development toward the beginning of the farmland that spread out over much of the valley. After traveling a few dozen yards, a black sedan came up from behind and slowed down next to them. Phil Porzinski rolled down his window and called out to the kids, "We're a little lost. Maybe you can help us out."

Dickie stopped pedaling and began coasting to a stop. NeNe caught up with him and whispered, "Dickie, you know we're not supposed to talk to strangers."

Dickie came to a stop, however, noticing the State of California seal posted on the passenger door of the sedan.

"If they offer us candy, I'm scramming," NeNe hissed as she braked next to her brother.

"We'll try to be of help, sir," Dickie said politely as he gave NeNe a slight jab in the ribs to keep her quiet.

Smiling amiably, Porzinski asked, "Do you know where Oaktree Lane is?"

NeNe was about to offer directions when Dickie elbowed her a second time and broke in, "Yes, sir." Pointing over his shoulder, he told Porzinski, "You go back the way you came and then turn left at the end of this road. Then you just keep going till you see the sign."

"How far?" Porzinski asked.

"Pretty far," Dickie said, matching Porzinski's smile with one of his own. "Just keep going south."

Porzinski frowned and glanced down at his clipboard a moment, double-checking his information. "I thought Oaktree Lane was in the Country Estates."

"It is, sir," Dickie explained. "They own a second piece of land outside Ramona. I directed another man there just yesterday."

"Okay," Porzinski replied, starting to roll his window back up. "Thanks."

"He was nice enough to give me a quarter," Dickie said, still smiling.

Porzinski snorted, turning his smile into a smirk as he reached into his pockets. He told Dickie, "You're pretty shrewd for your age, you know that?"

"Thank you very much, sir."

Porzinski flipped a coin at Dickie while Sloman shifted the sedan into gear and turned around. As the car sped off the way it had come, Dickie looked at the coin and muttered, "Hey, just a lousy dime! That creep!"

"Dickie," NeNe said as they started off. "You sent them to—"

"I know where I sent 'em," Dickie interrupted. His expression had changed quickly to one of concern. "Those guys were Feds! Come on, we gotta hurry home and implement Condition Red!"

Three

Phil Porzinski tapped out his last cigarette and angrily crumpled the pack in his hand. He tossed it on the floor as he stabbed his finger at the dashboard lighter, snarling, "I think that kid pulled a fast one on us, Sloman. Hell, we've been driving for almost an hour now. . . ."

"Well, he *did* say it was far away," Sloman ventured, fidgeting with his visor to help block out the glare of the sun as it dropped toward the western horizon.

"Yeah, well, I think he was lying to us from the word go." Porzinski flipped through the notes on the clipboard, blinking away the smoke that trailed up into his eyes. "It says here the address is in Ramona. Period. Hell, what did we—"

"Holy Hannah!" Sloman cried out suddenly, slamming on his brakes. "I don't believe it!"

Porzinski hadn't anticipated Sloman braking the car so abruptly, and he lunged forward, dropping his cigarette as he grabbed the dashboard to keep from going through the windshield. When hot ash began burning through his suit pants, Porzinski began bouncing recklessly about in his seat, trying to shake the cigarette off his lap as he swore a steady stream of profanities.

Up ahead, four lanes of cars were lined up before a massive gateway. Uniformed police were stepping out of small booths to converse with the drivers of each car. A large sign above the gateway informed Sloman and Porzinski that Dickie Cessna's directions had led them to the border between California and Mexico.

"Looks like you were right," Sloman observed, forcing a grin as he looked over at his partner, who was settling back in his seat and rubbing at the spot where the cigarette had ruined his pants. "Hey, what'd I tell you about smoking being dangerous?"

"Shut up and turn this thing around," Porzinski snapped.

"Sure thing, Phil," Sloman said, swerving off to the shoulder and waiting for traffic to pass before wheeling the sedan around and heading back for Ramona.

"That little shit," Porzinski seethed, straightening out his crumpled cigarette and jabbing it into his mouth. "I'd give anything for a chance to get my hands on him."

"Oh, come on, Phil. It was kind of a nice ride, don't you think? Real peaceful, like trips my folks used to take me on back when I was a kid. Shoot, I almost feel like he did—"

"Just shut up and drive, Mel, would you?" Porzinski shouted.

"You got it, Phil." Sloman pressed down on the accelerator, picking up speed. After a mile or so, he glanced over at his partner, who was still fingering the hole in his pants. "Look on the bright side, Phil. You could have dropped it on your crotch and wound up with roasted nuts, right?"

Porzinski slowly turned his head, taking in Sloman with a scowl of unbridled contempt. "My God, are you a sad case. Is this your second career after bombing out on vaudeville or something?"

"Just trying to keep things on the upbeat, Phil."

"Well, maybe I don't want to feel upbeat, Mel. Did you ever think of that? Maybe I want to stew in this nice rotten mood I've worked up. You want to feel upbeat, think about your frigging rides in the country with your frigging Mommy and Daddy, but do me a favor and keep it to yourself, okay?"

"Whatever you say, Phil."

They drove the rest of the way back to Ramona in silence, stopping briefly at a quick-stop service station for gas, cigarettes, and two chili dogs to go. By the time they were back on the same stretch of road where Dickie had led them astray, it was dark and Phil Porzinski was suffering from indigestion. He groaned as he looked over a map of the area under the dim light of the overhead lamp, trying to find their destination. Sloman was still behind the wheel, driving slowly as they passed by the various side streets shooting off the main road. Finally he blinked on his brights and flashed his turn signal, telling Porzinski, "I think I just found it."

"Finally," Porzinski said, setting down his map and looking out the windshield. "Oaktree Lane. Hallelujah . . ."

"Funny thing, though," Sloman commented, pulling off

to the side of the road just before the turnoff. "We drove by here this afternoon and I don't remember seeing any sign."

"Hey, that's funny, all right," Porzinski drawled sarcastically, lighting up another cigarette. "Mel, the day's been long enough. Turn the goddamn wheel, will ya?"

Sloman cornered the sedan and drove down the side road, which led away from the newer developments and into the rural outskirts of the small town.

"Okay," Porzinski said, his spirits picking up slightly, the way a wolf snaps out of the doldrums when it gets a whiff of blood in the wind. "Look for a big house. Cessna probably took all the money he owes us and bought himself a castle."

"We'll soon find out," Sloman said, checking the side of the road and soon spotting a hand-painted sign rising above the weeds. "Fifteen twenty-three. That's it, isn't it?"

"Sure is."

Sloman turned into the driveway and the sedan's headlights swept across an unkempt lawn before beaming onto the large, bulky frame of a weathered building just ahead. Painted over the entranceway facing them was 1523, lit by a single lightbulb that was almost completely engulfed by flies.

"Looks more like a barn than a castle," Sloman said, stopping the car and turning off the engine.

"Cessna's too smart to have anything plush on the outside," Porzinski hypothesized as he got out of the car. "Let's go. We've come a long way to nail this clown."

As Sloman followed Porzinski toward the building, he sniffed the air and said, "Smells like the farm I grew up on, you know? Gosh, what a day for memories, huh?"

"It's a day for forgetting, if you ask me," Porzinski complained, checking his pants to make sure the cigarette burn didn't show too badly. When he reached the faded oak door, he rapped on it harshly several times, then stepped back to survey the building closer. "Must be a converted stable."

From the other side of the door came a loud whinny and the slight clopping of hooves on hay.

"Sounds like it's not converted yet," Sloman said.

They were about to circle around to see if there was a main house located behind the stables when the oak door suddenly creaked open. A pale, fragile face peered out at them. It was a girl, fifteen at the oldest, her eyes red from weeping. She was wearing a tattered frock that ballooned outward beneath her breasts, making her look as if she were ready to go into labor at any second.

"Yes?" she sniffed, rubbing at her eyes with the back of her grimy hand.

Sloman flinched at the sight of the young woman. Porzinski cleared his throat and asked, "Mrs. Cessna . . . ?"

Shaking her head, the girl whispered, "No, I'm her daughter, June." Blinking back a few more tears, she added, "My parents are out. Can I help you?"

Sloman's eyes were fixed on June's rounded belly, and his face was etched with growing sadness. "No, that's all right," he said, nudging Porzinski. "We'll just be on—"

"No, wait," Porzinski said, discreetly shoving his partner's hand away. Determined to see his assignment through, he forged ahead in an official tone, "I'm Phillip Porzinski and this is Mel Sloman. We're from the Board of Taxation in San Diego."

"San Diego!" June gasped, a flicker of life creeping into her eyes. She stepped forward, reaching out for Porzinski as she stared hopefully into his eyes, asking, "Do you know a sailor named Bill? He said he'd be back from Thailand in the spring. . . ."

Sloman and Porzinski traded wary glances, and June retreated to the doorway, hope fading from her face. Another girl, four years her junior, appeared next to her and stared demurely at the two officers. She was dressed just as poorly as June, but at least she didn't look as if she were in the advanced stages of pregnancy.

"I'm Bette Cessna," she introduced herself. "You wanna come in and wait till my folks get home?"

"No, honey," Sloman said fumbling awkwardly with his plaid tie. "I think we've seen as much as we have to for—"

"As a matter of fact," Porzinski cut in, taking a step toward the door and looking past the children suspiciously, "we will come inside, thank you."

Ignoring Sloman's disapproving frown, Porzinski waited for June and Bette to step aside, then strode past them into the stable. Sloman hesitated.

"It's okay, you can come in," Bette said graciously. "Just remember, you took us a little by surprise, so the place isn't tidied up as much as it is normally."

Inside, the stables looked and smelled as if their principal tenants were still horses. More than a hundred of them could be heard stirring in their stalls, which lined either side of a main walkway running the length of the building. A kerosene lamp provided light in those places not reached by the bulb hanging from the center of the enclosure. Hay was strewn across the floor, but bare earth still showed through in places. Amid the riding gear and feedsacks, there were a few human touches that hinted that the stables served a secondary function. A few tacky paintings that looked as if they'd been rejected by a supermarket art department were hanging from rusty nails on one wall, along with an unframed family portrait. In the same clearing, there were plaques reading HOME SWEET HOME and NO SMOKING and a few kitchen utensils hanging from a broad beam. On the ground was a threadbare tablecloth draped over a stack of two hay bales. More bales were set like benches on either side of the would-be table.

"Good God . . ." Sloman mumbled pathetically as he took in the area.

"Would you like something to eat?" Bette said politely as her sister dabbed at her face with a handkerchief. "We have oatmeal, puffed oats, oat pudding. . . ."

"We've already eaten, honey," Sloman assured her. Leaning to one side, he pleaded to his partner, "Phil. Please."

Porzinski saw Sloman gesturing toward the door, but he gave a stiff shake of his head and continued staring at the interior of the stables, still suspicious. Smiling at Bette, he asked, "Would you mind giving us a little tour of your . . . home?"

"Not at all," Bette said, starting down the rows of stalls. Porzinski was immediately behind her, but Sloman followed only with great reluctance. June walked beside him, still sniffling.

As she pointed to handmade nameplates nailed above the individual stalls, Bette expounded like a veteran docent. "These are all our stalls. This is Big Red . . . Buttercup . . . Blackjack . . . My little sister NeNe and my brother Dickie . . . Slowpoke . . ."

"Wait a second," Sloman said, wandering over to the stall beneath the nameplate reading 'DICKIE AND NENE.' Porzinski joined him and they both peered in, barely able to make out the reclining figures of the two children, who were sleeping in fetal positions, half-buried by a layer of hay, each one facing a separate wall of the stall so that neither of the men could get a good look at their faces.

"You children *sleep* in there?" Sloman asked, incredulous.

"Dickie and NeNe do," Bette explained. "Me and June have that one over there."

As Bette pointed across the way, June whispered hoarsely, "But I'm getting my own stall when I have my . . . my . . ."

Unable to finish the sentence, June buried her face in her handkerchief. Bette came over and put an arm around her as she looked up at the two men, who watched with amazement.

"That's about it for the tour," Bette said meekly. "Unless you want to see more horses or the manure pile. . . ."

Sloman had reached the limit of his tolerance. Stepping in front of his partner, he told Bette, "We've seen enough, sweetheart. We'll be heading back now." He looked at the stalls a final time, fighting back the emotion that was threatening to overpower him. With his voice on the verge of choking, he added, "You kids take care of yourselves."

Sloman started back for the stable door. Porzinski tried to head him off, insisting, under his breath, "Mel, don't be in such a hurry to go along with whatever these—"

"Mr. Porzinski!" June called out, hurrying to catch up with the men. Taking Porzinski by the arm, she looked up at him with tears pouring freely down her face. "Please, could you look for Bill? I can't remember the full name of the ship, but I know the first three letters were U.S.S."

Porzinski stared down at the trembling hand that clutched at his arm, then looked over at Sloman, who was nodding his head forcefully at him. With a sigh, he pried June's fingers from his suit and said, "Okay, kid. Sure."

"Oh, thank you!" June gushed, leaning forward and giving the man an awkward hug. Porzinski shrank back from the embrace, beginning to shake himself.

"It was nice to meet you," Bette said, going to the door and opening it for the men. To her surprise, though, her mother and father were outside, just about to open the door themselves. They were both in their midforties, wearing mud-spattered coveralls that told of their day's work in the fields. Mr. Cessna was tall and barrel-chested. His wife was blond and petite, with sharp, tanned features.

"Bette! What in tarnation . . . ?" Mr. Cessna blurted out as he stepped inside. Spotting the two other men, he frowned, even more shocked. "Porzinski!? Sloman!?"

"Hello, Cessna," Porzinski said coldly. He nodded a curt greeting to the man's wife.

As they surveyed the stables, both Mr. and Mrs. Cessna's mouths hung open with astonishment. When they spotted June, with her stomach bloating outward, Mrs. Cessna looked as if she were about to faint.

"What's going on here?" Mr. Cessna demanded.

"We just wanted a look at your new surroundings, Mr. Cessna," Sloman explained apologetically.

"And they were just leaving, Daddy," Bette said, winking desperately at her parents as if there were springs on her eyelashes.

As the entire group left the building and headed toward the parked sedan, Sloman took Mr. Cessna aside and told him confidentially, "We'll report your present circumstances back to the Board. Just make payments as you're able to, and don't worry."

Mr. Cessna was still having trouble making sense of the situation, but he wasn't about to refute Sloman. His wife kept looking at June's belly. June signaled for her mother to go along with what was happening, then circled around the car, where Porzinski was climbing into the passenger seat, an unsatisfied scowl stamped across his face.

"Don't forget Bill!" she urged him. Lowering her voice, she added, "If it's any help, we met at the Holiday Inn across from the base. He had short hair and a tattoo on his right arm."

Porzinski looked away from her, staring past Sloman, who was starting the engine, at Mr. Cessna. "I'll be back," he promised grimly.

Standing next to her father, Bette waved and called out, "Let us know ahead of time and we can fix you up a guest stall."

Sloman smiled and waved back while Porzinski reached into his shirt pocket for his cigarettes. The sedan backed out of the driveway, then headed toward the main road. Mr. Cessna watched the retreating taillights a moment, then turned to June and Bette. Before he could begin to ask them the meaning of what had just happened, Dickie and NeNe came bursting out of the stable, dusting loose straw from themselves.

"We did it!" Dickie shouted excitedly.

Bette yanked off her ragged dress to reveal a T-shirt and shorts underneath. June did the same, then unstrapped the pillow that was bulging at her midsection. Tossing the pillow playfully at Dickie, she laughed, "So long, Junior!"

The kids' parents were slowly beginning to realize what had just transpired, and neither one of them seemed to be pleased with the implications.

"All right!" Mr. Cessna said, eyeing his children sternly. "Just how did this masquerade come about?"

Bette, June and NeNe all looked at their brother, and Dickie smiled sheepishly at the attention.

"Well, Dad, I can explain everything," he told his father.

"Good," Mr. Cessna said grimly. "I can't wait to hear it."

"Yes, this should be very interesting," Dickie's mother said with equal grimness.

As they came to the main road, Porzinski blew a thick cloud of smoke and said, "I smell a rat."

"All I could smell was horses," Sloman said.

"One more flimsy joke out of you, Mel, and I'm going to use your ear for an ashtray."

"Oh, come on, Phil. Have a heart. My God, those people are going through hard times. Why can't you believe that?"

Porzinski crushed out his cigarette and rolled down the window to let some of the night air in. "Don't be such a fool, Sloman. I'm telling you, if I wasn't so sick of the sight of Ramona right now, I'd head back there and do a little spying until I found out more about what kind of wool those Cessnas are trying to pull over our eyes. Which reminds me . . . you owe me lunch."

Four

One of the things Dickie looked forward to most about weekends was the chance to sleep late. Monday through Friday, he was always up by seven o'clock at the latest so that he could ride to school before the first bell. Saturdays he liked to lounge in bed until midmorning, drifting in and out of sleep, concocting new schemes and trying to dream how they might pan out. This Saturday, however, the alarm buzzed him out of dreamland while it was still dark, and by the time he'd thrown on his work clothes and shoveled down a quick breakfast of Wheaties and raisins, the sun was just beginning to creep above the eastern Cuyamacas. Trudging out of the house, he hopped on his bike and rode the short distance to the stables, where he was under his father's orders to start in early on his weekend chores to make sure he had time to complete the tasks that had been added to his workload as punishment for his hijinks the day before.

After he'd taken down the assorted props that had been used to mislead the tax agents, he began the thankless task of going from stall to stall and cleaning out manure the horses had left on the ground.

"Hey, thanks a lot, Slowpoke," he grumbled at the old roan in one of the first stalls as he held his breath and swept up a fresh deposit. "I'll remember this next time you're looking for someone to ride you."

Slowpoke was munching fresh oats from its feeding trough and paid no attention to Dickie. Most of the other horses were also eating, and their lack of attention to Dickie only made the job more unbearable. The rising sun threw scattered beams of light through the slats of the stables, warming the air. Once he'd cleaned out all the stalls, Dickie had a sizable collection of manure piled high on a small handcart, which he wheeled outside into the corral, where a dozen other steeds had scattered even more of their potent pies. Compared to the inside of the stables, though, the air was cleaner and less choked with flies. Trying to whistle his way into better spirits, Dickie began chasing down the separate clumps of manure and pitching them all together in one large pile. As if the horses had been conspiring with one another to add to Dickie's misery, they almost all seemed to be overcome with the urge to relieve themselves, usually in an area he'd just finished cleaning.

"Hey, knock it off, you guys!" Dickie yelled at them with irritation as he swept up one of the fresh deposits. "What did I ever do to you to deserve this anyway, huh?"

Once he had all the manure gathered together, he still

had to load it into the cart and then take it out of the corral to the huge pile collecting on the far side of the stables, upwind from the main grounds of the equestrian center, which his father ran in conjunction with the newly developing San Diego Country Estates. Mr. Cessna had been named general manager of the facilities a little over a year ago, shortly before they'd moved into one of the new Estate homes from their former house, located farther out in the country.

As he donned a pair of rubber boots and waded into the thick of the accumulating manure and began building up the main pile, Dickie tried to console himself with strange fantasies, the most common one being that he was standing on the rooftop overhead and forcing Harvey Peterjohn to walk a plank that extended over the manure pile. Harvey begged for mercy, but Dickie only laughed as he prodded him over the edge so that Harvey landed up to his neck in horseshit. The fantasy, however, did little to dispel the reality that it was he, Dickie, who was wading through the waste, swatting futilely at swarming flies and almost gagging as he tried to breathe only through his mouth.

The beating of the morning sun seemed to be activating more odors with each passing second. Dickie had spent almost all his life surrounded by horses, and many of his childhood memories were fondly highlighted by incidents that had to do with the four-legged creatures, but as the day wore on, he began to find himself wishing that he could string all of the center's horses and lead them to the nearest glue factory.

Dickie was finishing his third trip to the main manure pile when his father came riding up on a trim-looking mare. Richard Senior watched his son a few moments, then called out, "All right, Dickie."

Dickie straightened up, stabbing the tip of his shovel into the manure and looking over at his father. "I have more to do still," he said sullenly.

"You've suffered enough," his father told him. "Come on, one of the colts got loose. Give me a hand tracking it down."

Dickie didn't need a second invitation. Wading out of the manure pit, he quickly kicked off his boots and slipped into his tennis shoes, then went back into the stables to saddle up Buttercup, a caramel-colored steed with a flowing white mane. He led the horse out of the stable, then mounted and snapped the reins, following his father past the huge track, where a few owners were out watching their thoroughbreds run through their paces. As they headed into the foothills and began scouting the terrain for the errant colt, Mr. Cessna told his son, "I don't enjoy giving you pen duty, Dickie, but when you behave like you did yesterday you don't give me much choice. It was bad enough you got yourself and NeNe in trouble at school. Talking your sisters into helping you deliberately deceive government agents, well . . ."

"But, Pop," Dickie protested, spurring Buttercup on to keep up with his father. "Last week you said those guys were—"

"Okay, so maybe I *did* call them a few names I shouldn't have," Mr. Cessna interrupted quickly. "I didn't know you were listening in on your mother and me when we were discussing them."

"You were discussing pretty loudly," Dickie said. "I couldn't help but hear."

"Be that as it may, I still intend to play by the rules," Mr. Cessna said, reining his horse to a halt atop a ridgeline affording a view of the rolling Estates and the adjacent town. "If I wind up losing my case, heaven forbid, I'll pay those tax boys everything they think I owe them. It's my responsibility . . . Aha! Look, just ahead. There's the colt!"

Down the other side of the ridge, the spindly-legged colt was moving slowly along the roaming fence that separated the equestrian center from the rest of the hill country. Riding side-by-side, Dickie and his father coaxed their horses down to the fence, boxing the colt in. It made no effort to break away as Mr. Cessna dismounted and deftly flung a lasso over its head. As the loop tightened, the colt made as if to stagger away, but Mr. Cessna quickly drew in the excess rope and reached the animal's side, calming it by stroking its mane. Dickie hopped down from Buttercup and came over to assist.

"You have responsibilities, too, Dickie," Mr. Cessna said, slipping the loop off the colt's neck and quickly untying the slip knot. "To NeNe . . ."

"She gets twenty percent!" Dickie said.

"She also gets suspended from school, thanks to you." Mr. Cessna handed his son the rope. "Here, show me how you make a halter with this."

As he formed a new loop, Dickie said, "I'm sorry about that, Dad... but I think school's overrated. I mean, we go there and study about guys like Ford and Rockefeller who dropped *outta* school to make millions!"

Watching his son retie the slip knot, Mr. Cessna smiled and said, "Dickie, have you ever heard of the term 'hare-brained logic'?"

"You always tell me when I want something that I should 'find a way' instead of just wishing for it," Dickie maintained, sticking to his guns. "Well, I wanted to make some extra money, and that keno game was perfect!"

"Not if it broke school rules," Mr. Cessna countered. "Dickie, you've got to stop fleecing your classmates in keno games and numbers rackets. Start showing them a little respect. Understand?"

Dickie sighed dejectedly as he slipped the loop back over the colt's nose.

"Even Harvey Peterjohn?" he asked glumly.

"Even Harvey Peterjohn."

"Sheesh." Dickie tied the other end of the rope around his saddlehorn, then remounted with his father and began leading the colt back to the stables.

"I know you're bursting with ideas, son," Mr. Cessna said as they rode, seeing Dickie's downhearted expression. "But you've got to learn which ones to use and which ones to let drop."

"Yes, sir," Dickie murmured, staring straight ahead. Another of those ideas was in the process of bursting inside his head. He tried not to let on.

"Now, can I have your promise you won't cook up any more schemes at school?"

Dickie's features slowly changed from depression to inspiration. As they cleared the last of the foothills and began picking up their pace across the flatlands leading back to the center, he finally nodded his head and pledged, "Okay, Dad. I promise. No more schemes... at school."

"Well, I'm certainly glad to hear that. I'm sure Mr. Ruggles will, too, once your suspension is over."

"It's like you were saying, Dad," Dickie said, now grinning with anticipation at his latest brainstorm. "I just have to know which ideas are worth pursuing and stick to those, right?"

"Right, son."

Once they were back at the stables, Dickie dismounted and started to lead the colt into the corral. He paused at the gate and looked back at his father.

"Dad, do I have to do pen duty tomorrow, too?"

"I'll give it some thought. Why, do you have something planned?"

"Oh, I was just thinking of going over to the golf course, that's all . . ."

"Since when were you interested in golf, son?" Mr. Cessna asked.

"Just recently, Dad," Dickie said with a grin. "Just recently."

Five

The fairway for the fourth hole at the Country Estates Golf Course was flanked on both sides by a forest thick enough to hide several bands of Robin Hood's Merry Men. Not unsurprisingly, it was widely acknowledged among local duffers as The Curse of the Front Nine, since anything but a long, straight shot invariably resulted in one's golf ball vanishing into the dense woods, never to be seen again.

"Never fear, my dear," an overweight man in a garishly printed sport shirt assured his wife as he set his ball down on the tee and stared out at the thin strip of fairway before him. He was clearly trying to do an impression of W. C. Fields, but his voice more closely resembled Harry Reasoner with a sinus problem. "I shall negotiate the straight and narrow with my trusty three wood."

"William, use one of your shag balls, please," his equally plump wife urged him from her perch on the nearby golf cart.

William chortled confidently as he dug his cleats into the close-cropped grass and took a few light, practice swings with his club. "Cursed be thou of little faith."

"You just bought that ball half an hour ago," the woman

said, propping her sunglasses on her forehead. "You haven't even had a chance to get to know it and now you want to kiss it goodbye."

"Tsk tsk," the husband scolded, wagging a finger at his wife. "Negative attitude, dearest. We can't have that. . . ."

"Oh, honestly, William. . . ."

William lined up his shot, took one last practice swing, then cocked his three wood back and brought it around in a smooth, sweeping arc. The club's face kissed the ball with a sweet thwack and sent it rocketing toward the distant green.

Dropping her sunglasses over her eyes, William's wife quickly picked up the flight of the ball, a vindictive smirk curling the corners of her mouth. "It's hooking, William," she said. "What did I tell you . . . ?"

As the ball continued to swerve off course and toward the edge of the woods, William leaned the other way and made frantic gestures with his arms, trying to will the shot to land on the fairway. Out of the side of his mouth he chastised his wife, "It was your negative attitude that did it, woman. . . ."

"Hogwash, William," his wife huffed.

The ball dipped suddenly and seemed as if it were going to land in the fairway after all. However, there was a stirring in the brush and a diminutive figure abruptly burst forth from the woods, snatching the ball on the fly in a large catcher's mitt.

"What in blazes . . . ?" William gasped, blinking his eyes with disbelief. As he and his wife watched, the figure ducked back into the forest, disappearing as quickly as it had appeared.

William looked over at his wife, who slowly removed her sunglasses and even more slowly turned to him. Pointing down the fairway, she steadfastly insisted, "*That* was *not* my negative attitude, William. . . ."

The other side of the woods overlooked not only the eighth hole, but also a bending creek that ran through the golf course. Harvey Peterjohn, the skinny snitch who had blown the whistle on Dickie's keno empire, was kneeling at the edge of the creek's embankment, probing the running waters with a nine iron, stirring up sediment as he tried to find the ball he'd sent rolling off the rough moments before. Behind him, his father watched with increasing impatience. Orville Peterjohn was a crusty man in his midfifties, wearing an expensive three-piece outfit of tweed that might have been fashionable on the links a few decades ago.

"Are you looking for a ball or stirring a cauldron?" Orville asked his son as he tugged on the brim of his cap. "I brought you here to teach you how to golf, not fish."

"Just a sec," Harvey said, staring into the murky depths, waiting for the water to clear.

"Nothing doing," Orville spat, leaning over and grabbing Harvey by the earlobe.

"Yeoooooow! Daaaaad!" Harvey whined, struggling to his feet.

"Harvey, I've told you to keep your eye on the ball!" Orville lectured, waving his putter for emphasis. "They don't grow on trees!"

As Harvey rubbed the ear his father had grabbed, a squat, homely bulldog jumped down from their golf cart and waddled over to the edge of the creek. Poking its wrinkled face toward the surface of the water, it began to bark.

"Brutus thinks it's in here, too," Harvey defended himself.

"Brutus is probably commenting on your backswing!" Orville asserted. "You've cost me enough money today; from now on, you just caddy!"

Mr. Peterjohn strutted back to his cart with Brutus lumbering along beside him. Harvey lingered behind a moment, burning with shame, then timidly brought up the rear, bowing his head forlornly.

Moments after the threesome had sputtered off down the fairway, there was a slight splashing in the creek. Its only source at first seemed to be the raised tip of a dime-store snorkel, but soon a cartoonish-looking rubber turtle surfaced and began skimming along the ripples of the stream. Then the turtle itself sprang into the air, revealing beneath it the head and upper torso of NeNe Cessna, who was wearing a one-piece wetsuit. Clutched in her hand was a gleaming white golf ball, and when she took off her goggles and inspected her catch, she smiled at the sight of the Peterjohn name stamped on the side of the ball. As a gust of wind swept across the stream, NeNe shivered and chattered her teeth as she reached down into the creek, removing a net that was bulging with more golf balls. She was adding her latest acquisition to the collection when Dickie came rushing forth from the woods, still wearing his catcher's mitt. His pockets were filled to the point of bursting with still more balls.

"NeNe!" he called out excitedly. "How many did you get so far?"

Holding up her trove for Dickie to see, NeNe said, "Twenty-three." Sneezing, she added, "And one case of pneumonia!"

Dickie came over and helped his sister ashore, then pulled off his shirt and draped it over her shoulders. Two golf balls dribbled out of one of the pockets, missing his toes by inches and almost rolling into the stream before he was able to snatch them back up.

NeNe sneezed again, then rubbed her nose with the back of her hand as she sniffled, "I shoulda stayed retired."

"Come on, this is the best deal I ever offered you," Dickie told her. "Equal partners!"

"Equal punishment is more like it," NeNe sulked.

"Ahhhh, it's just a small price to pay," Dickie said, taking the filled net from her and slinging it over his shoulder. "It's in the bag! Just look at it this way; we're like gold prospectors who just panned a sack full of nuggets. Now all we gotta do is turn the stuff in and get our money!"

"Prospectors never had to snorkel for gold," NeNe complained, stepping out of her flippers.

"They never came up with this big of a payload, either," Dickie said cheerfully.

Six

Jim Clark lorded over San Diego Country Estates from his office on the second floor of the rustic guest lodge located next to the golf shop. It was a large, paneled office, filled with scale models of both existing and future projects. Blueprints hung from the walls, framed like works of art. An enormous picture window overlooked the golf course, and Clark stared out at players teeing off at the first hole as he listened to someone talking to him on the phone. He'd just turned fifty a month ago, but the strains of his job made him look a few years older. Dark pockets hung below his eyes, and his face was creased with wrinkles that distorted his features into an expression of constant harassment.

"Morton, I'm paying you to get *rid* of the damn gophers! From the looks of things it looks more like you're *breeding* them!" Clark shifted the phone to his other ear and rolled up his sleeves as he listened to his groundskeeper's latest excuse. When he'd heard enough, he cut in, "Morton, the eighteenth green has *three* holes! Now, you wipe those little buggers out, or I'm gonna dig a hole myself and stick you in it!"

Slamming down the phone, Clark pushed away from his desk, leaned back in his leather chair, crossed his legs and stared at the ceiling, looking as if he were appealing to the gods to smite Morton and the gophers with a bolt of lightning. His invocation was interrupted when Florence, his gray-haired secretary, stepped into the office.

"Richard Cessna's here to see you, Mr. Clark."

"Don't tell me the riding stable's screwing up, too!" Clark snarled, loosening his tie.

"Richard Cessna, Junior," Florence corrected herself. "He's here with his sister, Jeannine."

Clark threw his arms up with exasperation. "Florence, I've got a three-thousand-acre development to take care of. Just buy a couple raffle tickets or whatever it is they're pushing, and send them on their way. . . ."

The door behind Florence opened wider and the two Cessna children staggered into the room, lugging between them a bushel basket filled with golf balls. NeNe was still wearing her wetsuit, but she'd given Dickie back his shirt.

"It's not a raffle," Dickie groaned as they set down the basket and gasped for breath. They stood upright and rubbed at the indentations in their fingers made by the wire handles. "It's a service!"

A few of the golf balls rolled over the rim of the basket and landed on the floor. As Dickie and NeNe crouched to pick them up, Clark held out his hand and said, "Hold it! Just where'd you get all those golf balls!"

"They're all over, sir," Dickie explained, starting into an obviously rehearsed speech. "Golfers are too lazy to crawl after lost balls, but me and my assistant—"

"Ahem!" NeNe coughed, shooting Dickie a reproachful look.

Amending himself, Dickie went on, "But me and my *partner* are kids, and we enjoy doing it! We know you need used golf balls for the driving range, so we thought we'd show you how many we could collect in a week and then you'd be real impressed and put us on your payroll. Is it a deal?"

Clark leaned forward, propping his arms on his desk as he looked at the two children, who were watching him hopefully. Dickie had his catcher's mitt looped through his belt, and NeNe was carrying her snorkel and turtle headpiece, still sniffling from her runny nose. He wasn't sure what to make of them. Finally he gave his head a terse shake and informed the kids, "Okay, listen. I already pay a couple fellas—"

Before he could go on, there was a loud rap of knuckles on the office door. As Clark looked over at Florence questioningly, a voice called out, "Anybody home?"

Orville Peterjohn strolled into the office, followed by his son. Orville told Clark, "The clubhouse boy said you wanted to see me, Jim."

Spotting Dickie and NeNe, Harvey cracked, "Well, if it isn't the suspended Cessnas."

Dickie and NeNe both glared at their schoolmate while Orville walked up to Clark's desk. Clark sorted through the papers before him, finding the one he was looking for.

"That's right, Orville. There's a mistake in these new rates you sent me." Glancing over at the Cessnas, Clark said, "Let me just finish with these kids here and we'll—"

"There's no mistake," Orville said nonchalantly, smiling thinly.

"Orville," Clark retorted, waving the sheet. "This would mean a fifty percent increase."

Orville shrugged his shoulders. "My operating expenses have really mushroomed. I'm sorry, Jim."

Sensing that a confrontation was in the making, Florence turned to leave the office, almost stepping on Brutus, who waddled into the room, loudly sniffing at the carpet as it made its way to its master's side.

Clark put the paper down firmly and stared harshly at Orville, muttering, "I think the children better wait outside while we hash this out."

Orville put an arm around his son, drawing him close to his side. Sneering at Dickie and NeNe, he said, "I don't care about *those* children, but I encourage Harvey to listen to anything that has to do with my business. He is, after all, the heir to my fortune."

"We're in business, too," Dickie said, staying his ground and holding NeNe back from leaving the room.

Clark debated a moment, then told the Cessnas, "At least put your fingers in your ears."

"That's not a healthy thing to do," NeNe said. "The ear canal is a sensitive area, and when you stick something—"

"NeNe . . ." Dickie said, nudging his sister. He pressed his palms against the side of his head and gestured for NeNe to do the same.

Turning his attention back to Orville, Clark raised his voice, thumping his fist on his desktop. "Okay, you bullshitter! Why don't you just put on a mask and break into my safe!?"

"Hold on now, Jim," Orville said calmly. "Let's not be too hasty here. . . ."

"You're trying to rob me blind!" Clark shouted accusingly. "Just because you're the only fertilizer company in this whole goddamn town, you're not going to screw me royal! Got that?"

Grimacing at the language being hurled at his father, Harvey glanced down. His eyes fell on the bushel basket of golf balls and he quickly glanced up at Dickie, who just as quickly looked away.

"Harvey," Orville said, tightening his grip on Harvey's shoulder. "This is what we call a dissatisfied customer. Rather than take his abuse, what we do is tell him he's free to buy from a competitor . . . if he can find one. Come on, let's move along and take our business elsewhere."

Harvey was looking back at the bushel basket, and he suddenly grabbed one of the balls, blabbering, "Dad, look!"

"I said come on!" Orville said, tugging Harvey toward the door without looking to see that his son was pointing at their name stamped on the side of the ball. Dickie's hand shot out like a striking snake, snatching the ball from Harvey and tossing it back into the basket before covering his ears again.

"Brutus! Let's go!" Orville commanded, snapping his fingers at the bulldog, who was straddling a miniature putting green near the picture window. Before obeying the command, Brutus first responded to nature's call, darkening the artificial turf of the green with a small, yellow puddle.

As the Peterjohn clan hastily departed, Clark bolted from his chair to survey the damage, howling, "That mutt pissed on my putting green!" Pointing a warning finger at the closing door, he shouted at Orville, "I ought to take that disgusting dog and shove him up your rear, you swindler!"

Dickie and NeNe looked at one another, trying to keep straight faces. Clark stormed back to his seat and plopped down, jerking at his tie and running his hand through his hair as he tried to regain his composure before addressing the children.

"All right," he muttered gruffly. "Now, what was I saying?"

With her ears still covered, NeNe said, "'I ought to take that disgusting dog and shove him up your—'"

"I remember now," Clark interjected, staring at the bushel basket. "I was saying I already pay a couple fellas to take care of the golf course . . . and that includes looking for lost balls. So, if there aren't any balls for them to find, then I'm paying them for a job they can't do. In other words, each ball you have there is costing me around twenty cents in unearned salary to my employees." He paused, seeing Dickie and NeNe swallow hard at the import of what he was saying, then resumed, "Now, if you can grab that many balls in a week, in about two years you'd probably put me out of business. Then I couldn't lease my stables to your father, he'd be stuck with all his horses, he'd have to sell your house, and we'd all wind up out on the street. And since none of us wants that to happen, no deal."

Dickie was stunned. As he lowered his arms to his side and stared glumly at the balls they'd collected, NeNe looked at him and mocked, "'It's in the bag . . .'"

Shifting in his seat, Clark reached for his wallet, telling the children, "Now, before you leave, I guess the Estates owes you a little something for these balls you already rounded up. How many you got there?"

"Two hundred and thirty-two," Dickie droned sadly.

"Okay," Clark said, pulling out two ten dollar bills. "If I gave you each ten dollars, that'd be about ten cents a ball, right?"

"We don't do long division until next year," NeNe confessed.

Sighing, Dickie grabbed NeNe by the elbow and they both stepped up to the desk.

"We'll take it," he told the owner.

As he handed them the money, Clark advised, "And from now on, stick to the schoolyard and leave my golf course alone! Is that clear?"

"Yes, sir," Dickie said demurely.

"And remind your father he's supposed to clear out the manure that's been piling up by the stables. It's not my idea of a tourist attraction."

"Yes, sir," NeNe replied.

Disheartened, the children left the office and went to the bike racks, freeing their Stingrays and riding off in silence. Once they'd reached the main road, Dickie and NeNe stopped their bikes a moment to look back at the golf course through the fence bordering the property.

"Dickie, let's face it," NeNe said. "It's a grown-up's world. They own everything, they run everything . . . we're just here to mow the lawns."

Dickie grunted, only half-listening. His attention had drifted to the huge hydroseeder rolling along the shoulder of the road. Mounted on the truck's bed was a cylindrical tank, to which was attached an elaborate spray nozzle being operated by a workman standing at the rear. As the man aimed the nozzle over the fence and shouted a signal, the driver picked up the truck's speed slightly. Throwing a switch, the man in the back of the truck braced himself and held on tightly to the nozzle as a thick jet of green goo spewed forth, showering the hill on the other side of the fence.

"Let's go home, Dickie," NeNe said, mounting her bike and starting to pedal off behind the truck.

But Dickie was in the throes of another inspiration. Noting that the writing on the side of the tanker read PETERJOHN SEED AND FERTILIZER CORPORATION, he paid close attention to the task being performed, mumbling to his sister, "Nah, you go ahead. I want to watch 'em seed the banks for awhile . . . NeNe, look out!"

His warning came too late, though, and NeNe rode headlong into the path of the green spray shooting out of the tanker's nozzle. The man on the truck was standing in such a way that he couldn't see NeNe, and by the time he'd directed the discharge away from her, the young girl was covered completely with the unpleasant slime. Stopping her bike, NeNe looked down at herself and began to bawl.

"Hey, NeNe, are you all right?" Dickie shouted, racing over to her as she was wiping the residue from her face, still weeping. "Don't worry, sis, it's chemical fertilizer, not horse manure. . . ."

The news did little to console NeNe, who scraped another handful of the slop from the front of her wet suit and threw it fitfully at the retreating truck.

"Hey, wait a minute . . . !" Dickie said, his eyes lighting up.

"Oh, no," NeNe said flicking her fingers so that some of the fertilizer splattered in her brother's face. "If you've got another idea, keep it to yourself."

"NeNe, listen—"

"Look at me!" NeNe wailed. "This is what I got for listening to you one too many times already."

"But I can make it up to you if you just give me a chance!"

"Hah!" NeNe spat, getting back on her bike. "If I gave you a chance, you'd toss grass seed on me now and try to put me in a freak show. Forget it!"

As NeNe rode off, leaving a trail of fertilizer in her wake, Dickie looked over at the freshly seeded hills, mumbling to himself, "Just wait and see. Just wait and see!"

Seven

Now that turkeys were no longer the means to the town's notoriety, anyone looking for a new honor of dubious distinction to bestow on Ramona might have christened the place Gopher Capital of the World. The rodents terrorized not only the golf course, but also the vast majority of the residential area, including the new Country Estates. When Dickie pedaled his way home that afternoon, he found his father engaged in that one enterprise that rivaled mowing the lawn as the most frequently performed ritual outside the family's split-level home. Mr. Cessna was kneeling on the grass near the front flower beds, wiping aside tiny mounds of freshly dug earth to reveal the latest series of gopher holes dotting the landscape, which was visibly suffering from the presence of the underground varmints.

"Dad!" Dickie called out, pulling into the driveway and dropping the kickstand on his bike before rushing across the lawn to where Mr. Cessna was concentrating on the trap in his hand, delicately setting the spring mechanism and then slipping it into the hole.

"Hello, son," he said absently as he slowly pulled his hand free of the hole.

"Dad, what does your contract with the Country Estates say about manure?"

"It says it's my responsibility to get rid of it," Mr. Cessna said, pointing to the other holes pockmarking the lawn. "Dickie, some prankster's been springing my gopher traps."

Not paying any attention to his father's concern about the traps, Dickie ventured enthusiastically, "What if you... what if *I* wanted to keep it?"

"Keep what?" Mr. Cessna asked, wiping dirt from his hands.

"All the manure!"

Mr. Cessna looked up at Dickie and suggested, "Son, if you're looking for a hobby, you'd be better off collecting stamps." Baiting another trap, he shifted his position so that he could reach the next hole. "These pests are wrecking your mother's garden. You got any idea who's been fooling around with the traps?"

"No, Dad," Dickie said. "How many horses do we clean up after?"

After setting the trap in place, Mr. Cessna groaned his way to his feet and rubbed his lower back as he thought aloud, "All our riding horses... plus the show horses, and the race horses... I think it comes to a hundred and seventy-two. Why do you ask?"

Dickie was already juggling figures in his head. He whispered under his breath, "It's too big for just me and NeNe...."

"Dickie," Mr. Cessna said, eyeing his son skeptically. "Is

this another one of your schemes? That reminds me . . . your sister came home a few minutes ago looking like she'd taken a bath in cream of celery soup. Why do I get this feeling that you might have had a hand in that?"

"Nothing would have happened if she'd listened to me," Dickie defended himself. "I tried to warn her."

"Well, that's beside the point. I don't want to hear that you've cooked up some new way of getting yourselves into trouble. Remember, you promised me . . ."

"Don't worry, Pop," Dickie said brightly. "This one's on the up and up!"

As Dickie ran up the steps and disappeared inside the house, Mr. Cessna shook his head to himself and murmured, "My son, the snake-oil salesman."

NeNe was in her room, toweling her hair dry, when Dickie ran in, yelling, "NeNe! We're back in business!"

NeNe stared at him blankly, then said, "Excuse me. Do I know you?"

"Aw, come on, NeNe, don't be like that!"

"I'm sorry, I can't hear you," she said, turning away from him. "I have fertilizer in my ears!"

"NeNe, NeNe . . ." Dickie paced before the doorway as his sister finished with the towel and began folding it, acting as if he weren't there. "NeNe, I'm sorry."

"You sure are, Dickie. You're the sorriest excuse for a brother I ever heard of!"

"You don't mean that!"

"All you ever do is sucker me into your dumb plans and get me into trouble."

"This one's different!"

NeNe laughed bitterly. "Hah! That's what you always say. Go away. I don't want to listen to you any more, Dickie Cessna. Try your luck with Bette or June."

"I will," Dickie said. "But I wanted to give you the first crack. I owe you that much."

"Oh, spare me. . . ." NeNe rolled her eyes as she began combing her hair into a ponytail.

Dickie was about to give up when he hit on a new ploy. Reaching into his pocket, he pulled out the ten dollar bill he'd gotten from Mr. Clark and handed it to NeNe, saying, "Here. Take this and just listen to my plan. If you still think it's not worthwhile after I've finished, you can keep the money. Deal?"

NeNe looked at the bill waving in front of her face, then reached out and took it. Dickie didn't let go of it immediately, though.

"You didn't answer me," he said.

"Okay, I'll listen."

"Great!" Dickie said. "Come on, I'll tell you about it on the way to the stables."

"The stables?"

"Yeah," Dickie said. "Like I told you, I'm gonna want to get Bette in on this, too. I'm talking about large-scale family business here!"

Eight

Bette was attending to a middle-aged Japanese couple and their teenage daughter, who had come by the equestrian center to indulge themselves in an hour's worth of horseback riding along the various trails coursing through the Estates property. All three of the tourists were mounted up, wearing cowboy hats and Western outfits that were still creased with folds, having been purchased less than an hour before. As the father double-checked the three cameras dangling from his neck, Bette went from horse to horse, checking saddles and adjusting stirrups as she gave last-minute instructions to the daughter, who was the only one in the family who spoke English.

". . . All right, I think you're ready to start out," Bette said. "Remember, keep your feet in the stirrups and your hands on the reins and you won't have any problems."

While the other girl relayed the advice to her parents, Bette began walking the horses out of the corral. Just then, Dickie and NeNe came riding up on their bicycles.

"Bette!" Dickie called out, skidding his bike to a halt and laying it down as he ran over to the corral. "I gotta talk to you!"

"Dickie, can't you see I'm busy here?" Bette said indignantly.

Dickie looked at the tourists, greeting them with a polite nod as he sized them up. "Oh," he told Bette, speaking loud enough for the riders to hear. "Did you tell them about the deer trail?"

"Dickie!" Bette said, an angry gleam in her eye.

The young girl in the saddle took Dickie's bait, leaning over her saddle and asking him, "Excuse me. What trail?"

Coming up behind her brother, NeNe covered her mouth and pretended to cough in order to hide her laughter as Dickie pointed in the direction of the woods, telling the tourists, "We can start you out around that way, and there's a good chance you'll see wild deer feeding in the woods. It's only an extra dollar apiece . . ."

While the girl discussed the option with her parents, Bette snapped the reins she was holding at Dickie to get his attention.

"I don't believe you, Dickie," she whispered.

Dickie only smiled and shrugged his shoulders. Next to him, NeNe continued to have her coughing fit.

The Japanese daughter finished talking with her parents, then turned to Bette and said, "We'll take the deer trail, thank you."

"Look, to be honest," Bette said, "I don't think it's worth the extra money."

"Oh?"

When the girl related the opinion to her parents, the man bobbed his head affirmatively, smiling at Bette as he rattled off a sentence in his native tongue, pointing to his cameras.

"The deer trail," the daughter repeated on her father's behalf. "Please."

Letting out a sigh of displeasure, Bette began turning the horses around to face the trail her brother had pointed out. Dickie grabbed her by the arm and insisted, "Let NeNe do it. We gotta talk!"

Lowering her voice, Bette said, "Darn right we do, you creep!"

NeNe took the reins from Bette and led the tourists off. Once they were out of earshot, Bette turned on Dickie, warning him, "You know what Dad'll do if he finds out you're pulling that deer trail stunt again!?"

"In times of emergencies you have to take risks," Dickie

maintained. "Me and NeNe need every buck we can get for our new business. And we need you to come in with us!"

Bette shook her head and started walking off. "Dickie, I haven't recovered from *last* summer's losses . . . !"

"At least let me explain it to you!" Dickie said, catching up with her as they both headed down another trail that led into the woods.

"Save your breath," Bette told him. "I shouldn't even be helping you pull off this trick with the tourists, you know. You're making me an accomplice."

"A partner," Dickie corrected persistently. Reaching into his pocket, he pulled out the ten dollar bill NeNe had given back to him on their way to the stables. "Look, here's ten bucks. Take it and just listen to my plan. . . ."

Dickie had laid it all out for Bette by the time they reached an old tool shed just off one of the main trails and half-hidden by a clump of brush. As Bette twirled the dial on the combination lock linking the chain looped through the door handles, she thought over the plan and finally shook her head.

"I'm not interested, Dickie," she said as she popped the lock and withdrew the chain.

"Bette, this isn't some two-bit keno game!" Dickie said as he opened the doors of the shed and bent over to pick up something inside. "This is legit . . . and we can make a fortune!"

There was a thrashing in the nearby brush. Dickie and Bette looked over, spotting NeNe making her way toward them, whispering loudly, "Hurry, they're coming!"

Bette gave Dickie a hand, and together they hoisted up the large stuffed head of a moose, holding onto it by its outstretched antlers. The head was almost as large as NeNe, so it was with considerable difficulty that the three children carried it over to a nearby oak and fastened a loop of thick rope around its neck.

As he threw the other end of the rope around the lowest branch of the tree, then pulled down hard so that the moose's head was elevated to the height it would be if it were attached to a body, Dickie asked Bette, "So, what do you say, Bette?"

"Yeah," NeNe piped in. "You gonna go in with us, Bette?"

"N . . . O . . ." Bette spelled as she took the loose end of the rope and tied it securely around the trunk of the tree. "No!"

"Why not?" Dickie said, taking a long stick and fitting its tip into a notch on back of the mounted head so that he could not only steady it, but also maneuver it so that it would appear that the moose was bobbing its head to nibble at the thick bush that stood between the horse trail and the oak tree.

"Because," Bette explained impatiently. "I've already got chores to do each day, and I want to devote the rest of my time to getting good grades."

Dickie and NeNe groaned simultaneously, rolling their eyes.

"What kind of talk is that?" Dickie said.

"Look, jerk-off!" Bette snapped. "I want to be a doctor, and medical schools only take the best students!"

Before Dickie could lash back with a rejoinder, NeNe put a finger to her lips and shushed him into silence as she pointed through the brush. The children could hear the sound of approaching hooves, as well as a smattering of Japanese. NeNe hid by the shed while Dickie and Bette crouched next to one another behind the tree. Dickie kept his eye on the suspended moosehead as he jiggled his stick slightly, testing its mobility.

"Nitwit," he finally retorted, keeping his voice low. "It'll be twenty years before you can be a doctor!"

"So what?"

"So what?!" Dickie hissed, "You watch the news. . . . Neutron bombs! Nuclear plants! Pollution! What do you think the world'll be like in twenty years? I'll tell you! There won't be any air you can breathe; you won't have any gas for your car; all your food will be full of chemicals . . . Why wait around for *that*? Get the money *now*, while there's still some stuff you can spend it on!"

"Nice try, Dickie," Bette smirked, "but I think I'll take my chances."

"Shhhhhhh," NeNe warned from the shed.

From their place of hiding, Dickie and Bette could barely make out the advancing tourists, but the foreign voices carried clearly through the air, sounding above the clop of hooves. Bette tossed a handful of twigs and gravel at the bushes, and from the excited reaction of the tourists, it seemed obvious that their attention had been drawn to the moosehead, which was still far enough away from the trail that they couldn't tell that it wasn't alive. As Dickie carefully jostled the head to make it go through its eating motions, he grinned at the sound of clicking cameras in the distance.

"You're terrible, Dickie," Bette told him quietly. "I don't know why I went along with this."

"Because you know that I won't let you down in the long run," Dickie whispered. "Now, getting back to our new project..."

"*Your* new project."

"Listen, Bette, we can't do this without you."

"Try..."

Out on the horse trail, the Japanese family had stopped riding now, and they continued to converse enthusiastically as the father changed lenses on his cameras.

Deciding that he would have to resort to still another incentive if he hoped to get Bette to go along with his plan, Dickie whispered, "Listen, how would you like me to help you do something about the crush you have on Neil Brody?"

Bette's face turned red as she snapped, "That's a crock—"

"I read it in your diary," Dickie informed her calmly.

"I'll break your butt, you little snoop!"

"Shhhhh, quiet!" Dickie put his free hand over his sister's mouth as he looked to see if the tourists had been alerted by Bette's outbursts. He could only make out the tops of their heads, but it looked as if they were still engrossed with the swaying moosehead.

"How dare you?" Bette railed in a wrathful whisper.

"Hey, it's all for a good cause," Dickie said. "If you go in with us, I promise I can set you up with Neil."

Bette hesitated a moment and Dickie smiled slightly. He had her.

"How?" Bette wondered, a trace of sadness now in her voice. "He doesn't even know I'm alive."

"Look, Neil's the editor of the school paper, and what we're going to do would make a good story for him, right?" Dickie reasoned. "When he comes around asking for an interview, well, *somebody* would have to talk to him...."

Dickie let Bette dwell on that for a moment while he

shifted his position to keep his foot from falling asleep. At the same time, out on the trail one of the horses neighed loudly as the man with the cameras dismounted and began moving in through the brush for a closer shot.

"Understand," Bette finally said, "I still don't like the childish, two-bit stunts you've pulled in the past . . . but this is different. Count me in, but don't breathe a word about my diary to anyone! Especially Neil."

"I promise," Dickie said, elated. "Now give me my ten dollars back."

As he reached for the bill Bette was handing to him, Dickie took his eyes off the moosehead. The moment's distraction was all that was needed for the stick to slip free of its niche.

"Dickie!" NeNe cried out across the way, but the warning came too late. Swinging free of the stick, the moosehead began to spin slowly with the untwisting of the rope that still held it suspended in view of the tourists. Back on the trail, the wife of the cameraman screamed with shock at the sight while her husband blinked with wonder, then quickly raised one of his cameras to his face to snap a quick series of shots of the revolving head.

As he jumped to his feet and rushed over to steady the head, Dickie looked over at NeNe, demanding, "Hey, how come you let me do that!?"

"Me . . . ?" NeNe gasped.

Dickie was trying to fit the tip of his stick back into place when the Japanese father cleared his way through the bushes and came upon the three children. He looked at the disembodied head of the moose and pushed back the brim of his Stetson, looking like an Oriental sheriff who'd just caught the James Gang in the middle of a heist.

"Uh . . . hi!" Dickie said, embarrassed. "I guess maybe I should explain. . . ."

Nine

Now that Bette and NeNe had thrown in with Dickie's new top-secret project, there remained only one more recruitment, and Dickie decided that that night would be as good a time as any to tie up that last loose end. After supposedly going to bed for the night, he stayed up going over the preliminary paperwork on the project, trying to figure all the angles. Then, at a little after ten, he slipped on his bathrobe and sneaked out of his upstairs bedroom. Tiptoeing down the carpeted hallway, he came to the head of the stairs, where he encountered both NeNe and Bette, who were in their pajamas and hiding furtively behind the banister.

He crouched beside them and whispered, "Hey, what's the—"

"Shhh," NeNe whispered back, then silently gestured down the steps at the living room below.

June was sitting on the couch with her boyfriend, Frank Tebbets, an athletic-looking teenager fighting a losing battle with the physical urges of his adolescence. He had his arm around June's shoulder, and his hand was pretending to be a gopher, trying to find some way to burrow beneath her blouse. No longer made-up to look the part of a sickly, pregnant teenager, June radiated a blossoming beauty that further provoked Frank's glandular preoccupations.

"Mmmmmmm, you're so soft," he moaned in her ear, nuzzling close as his hand continued to rove.

"Fraaaaaank," June said, squirming from his embrace. Trying to take his mind off the moment's pursuits, she abruptly shifted the conversation and complained, "You promised we'd go to the drive-in tomorrow. . . ."

"I know, Juney," Frank said, sliding back to her side, "but I had to buy some parts for my car. I'm flat."

"Then just pretend I am, too," June huffed, pushing his hand away from her.

"Come on, Juney," Frank said, forging ahead and putting his arm around her. Smiling seductively, he leaned his lips close to hers and told her, "There's nothing we do at the drive-in that we can't do right here. . . ."

Satisfied that she'd put up her ration of token resistance, June closed her eyes and pursed her lips until they met with Frank's and became quickly and passionately acquainted. As Frank twisted around and began gently to guide June into a prone position, NeNe elbowed Bette at the top of the stairs and did an exaggerated impersonation of their older sister, puffing her lips out like a starving fish at feeding time and crossing her eyes as she put her arms around an imaginary Frank. Bette quickly clamped a hand over her own mouth to stifle a fit of giggles that threatened to blow their cover.

"Excuse me," Dickie whispered as he moved around NeNe and Bette to reach the steps. "We're gonna need June . . ."

Bette grabbed the sleeve of Dickie's bathrobe and shook her head. "Dickie, you're never gonna get June to join us!"

Grinning confidently, Dickie reminded her, "That's what NeNe said about you."

By the time Dickie reached the bottom of the steps, Frank looked like he had June down for the ten count in a wrestling match and was about to claim his winnings. Before he could uncover June's secret surprises, though, Dickie made his presence known, striding nonchalantly into the room as he sang, "*Tarzan, Tarzan man/He does something no one can* . . . oh, hi, June! Is that Frank with you?"

Frank jolted upright as if his errant fingers had wandered into an electrical socket. His face tried to camouflage itself with his red sweater as he glowered at their unannounced intruder.

"Dickie!" June shouted indignantly as she straightened her blouse. "Dad said you're not allowed out of your room! You scared those tourists back to Tokyo. . . ."

"I know," Dickie said, avoiding Frank's gaze. "But I gotta talk to you about something important."

"It can wait," June said.

"No it can't," Dickie insisted.

June wagged a warning finger at her brother and shouted, "Look, if you don't get out of here, you little worm, I'm—"

"Easy, June, easy," Frank said, regaining his composure

and holding her arm down. "Let me take care of this." As he reached into his jeans pocket for some change, he smiled endearingly at Dickie and said, "Listen, if you were to decide it's not so important after all . . . it could be worth a quarter to you!"

Frank held the coin up under Dickie's nose as if it were a magic amulet that would make him instantly disappear. Dickie looked at the quarter, a smirk creeping across his face.

"Really, now. . . ." He sighed pitifully, stuffing his hand into his bathrobe pocket. "Look, Frank, I heard June beefing about you being short of cash. Well, since I've been doing okay myself . . ." He pulled out the bill he'd used on NeNe and Bette and stuffed it in Frank's hand. ". . . here's a ten buck loan. Have a good time at the drive-in tomorrow, treat yourself to a little snack, too, maybe . . . but tonight I want to be left alone with my big sister. Okay?"

June stared at her brother suspiciously while Frank gaped at the ten dollar bill rubbing elbows with the quarter he'd tried to bribe Dickie with. "I can't take this," he finally said.

June whirled around and asked Frank, "You have other plans for paying for tomorrow night, huh?"

"But . . ." As Frank fumbled for his pride, Dickie grabbed his jacket from the armchair next to the couch and tossed it to him.

"Go ahead, Frank," June told him. "I want to see what this little rodent is up to."

Frank hesitated, getting used to the idea that his yearnings for the evening had just been thwarted. Once the bulge in his britches had subsided to the point where he could stand up without having to stoop to hide the evidence, he gave June a kiss and whispered, "I'll see you tomorrow."

Dickie had already moved to the front hall and opened the door for Frank. As the older teenager sulked past him, Dickie gave him a pat on the back and cheerfully advised him, "Don't do anything I'm not old enough to do."

Frank stopped in the doorway and warned Dickie, "Once I pay you back, I'm going to drop-kick you all the way to San Diego, you little smartass!"

"You have a nice night, too, Frank," Dickie said, closing the door.

"Okay, Dickie, what's going on?" June wanted to know as

soon as they were alone. "You've never given away money in your life!"

"And I'm not starting now," Dickie insisted. "It was a loan. Wait till I tell that bum my interest rates."

"He's not a bum," June said.

Pacing before the couch, Dickie lectured, "June, he's a *teenager.* He's smoking dope, he's got no job, he's got no motivation . . . his only dough is what his old man gives him and he blows all that on camshafts. You wanna wear his ring, you'll have to buy him some Cracker Jacks and hope its a lucky box. . . ."

Despite her anger, June couldn't help a brief snicker. Once it passed, she asked, "Why are you telling me all this?"

"Because you have a lot of vital needs." Dickie started counting them on his fingers. "New clothes, skin creams, record albums. Your allowance can't cover all that. And Frank's certainly no help. . . ."

Catching a glimpse of motion out of the corner of her eye, June looked over at the stairs, where NeNe and Bette were creeping not-so-stealthily down the steps. From their expressions, June began to suspect what was coming next, and she turned back to Dickie, determined to resist the inevitable.

"If you come in with *us,*" Dickie offered, nodding his head in the direction of his younger sisters, "we'll all be as rich as Orville Peterjohn!"

"What are you talking about?" June gasped mockingly. "Orville Peterjohn's the richest man in Ramona."

"Yeah!" Dickie said, as if that proved the point he was trying to make. "And how'd he get that way?"

"Selling fertilizer."

"Right again! And what do we throw away piles of, every day, no less?!"

June pieced it together as NeNe and Bette came over and stood with Dickie, hopefully watching for her reaction.

"Dickie, it can't be that simple. . . ."

Dickie laughed, "That's what they said to the guy who invented the Frisbee. . . ."

Ten

The arrival home of Mr. and Mrs. Cessna from their evening out brought an abrupt end to the first meeting of the new partnership. When the children reconvened the next day, it was in the converted activity room above the stables. Cluttered with stray belongings and bulky memorabilia from the family's two previous homes, the space had a chaotic air to it, and the sounds made by the horses in the stalls below further conspired to keep the discussion at hand from staying on a level of strictly business.

Presiding over the meeting from his perch atop an old-fashioned rolltop desk, Dickie looked at his sisters as he drove home his primary concern regarding their venture.

"Okay, we're going to be competing with a corporation, so first we ought to be a corporation ourselves. That means president, vice-president, secretary and what not. . . ."

June glanced over at her younger sisters and wisecracked, "I wonder what little big shot wants to be president... Dickie."

"Tricky Dicky," Bette laughed. "That seems to have a familiar ring to it."

"Very funny," Dickie said. "Okay, that's one nomination. Any others?" Before any of the girls could respond, Dickie went on, "Nominations are closed. I'd like to thank all my supporters . . ."

"Wait a minute!" Bette said, waving her hand to get everyone's attention. Getting up from the old hope chest she'd been sitting on, she eyed Dickie. "How come you get to be it? I get better grades."

"Hey, since when do presidents need brains?" Dickie said in his defense. "They just gotta be good front men who can give long speeches. And who's the best talker here . . . ?"

"Case closed," NeNe said.

"Thank you," Dickie told her. Addressing the others, he announced, "And for my vice-president, I pick NeNe!"

Having watched her share of political gatherings on television, NeNe stood up and bowed to imaginary applause, feigning shock and humility. "I don't know what to say!" she gushed. "This is all so sudden. . . ."

"Cut the shit, Dickie," Bette complained, ignoring NeNe's theatrics.

Seconding the opposition, June said, "I'm not going to be in some stupid corporation if you and NeNe are in charge, Dickie. . . ."

"What are you two griping about?" Dickie jumped down from the desk and began pacing. "Vice-president's a bozo job. All they do is cut ribbons and talk about how great the president is. You want to do that?"

June and Bette traded glances, then June spoke for them both. "Not on your life."

"I didn't think so." Dickie smiled at his youngest sister. "It's yours, NeNe."

"I'm no bozo. . . ." NeNe protested.

"Well, of course you're not," Dickie said, thinking fast. "That's why I gave the job to you, so you can make something out of it."

"Oh . . ."

While NeNe was busy trying to make sense of Dickie's double-talk, he went on to the next item on his agenda. "Next, we need a secretary."

"Bette's got the best handwriting," June said.

"Oh, no. Not me!" Bette shook her head vigorously. "I'm going to be a doctor so I don't get *stuck* being a secretary."

"What if we called it *executive* secretary?" Dickie bargained.

"It's still got *secretary* in it."

"So does secretary of state, and you don't see him bitching about it, do you?"

"He's got you there, Bette," June said.

While Bette reconsidered, Dickie pretended to pick up a phone and carry on a conversation with the editor of the school paper. " 'Hello? . . . You want an interview, Neil? Talk to our executive secretary!' What do you think of *that*, Bette? It's got heaps of dignity. C'mon, what do you say?"

Elsewhere in the room, NeNe and June nodded Bette's way. She finally took up the cue and shrugged. "I'll try it," she said, far from enthusiastic.

"Great!" Dickie went back to the desk, grabbing a pad

and pencil and then handing them to Bette. "Now start taking notes. June, since you're the oldest, you ought to get the job with the most responsibility. Even though teenagers aren't famous for their thrift, we'll make you treasurer."

"I can hardly wait," June said sarcastically. "I'll probably get stuck with all the bills if this thing falls through."

"C'mon, June, you can't talk like that!" Dickie exclaimed. "Forget all the other crap we've done in the past. That's all chump change stuff. We're talking big bucks here, and if we're gonna make it big, we gotta have the right attitude!"

"Well, if it isn't Dale Carnegie himself," June drawled.

"Who?" NeNe said, looking toward the doorway. "I don't see anyone. . . ."

"She's talking to me, NeNe," Dickie said. "Dale Carnegie's a famous guy who knew what it takes to be successful. Thanks for the compliment, June."

"Don't mention it . . . please."

"What are we going to call the corporation?" Bette asked.

"That's the next order of business," Dickie replied, pacing once again. "It should be something with a real ring to it. Something big . . ."

As the four officers mulled over the possibilities, the horses below neighed fitfully, almost as if they were laughing.

"I got one," Bette offered at last. After a dramatic pause, she said, "How about 'The Cessna Girls and Dickie'?"

"Hmmmmm," June mused. "That's kinda catchy."

"Are you kidding?" Dickie blurted out. "This is a business we're trying to put together here, not a circus act, for crying out loud!"

"You wouldn't be so bent out of shape if I'd have put your name first, I bet," Bette taunted her brother.

"Baloney," Dickie grumbled.

"Hey, I got it!" NeNe cried out excitedly. " 'The Shovel-Uppers'!"

"What?" Dickie said, tilting his head to one side and screwing his face up as if he'd just sucked on a lemon.

"We're going to *shovel up* manure," NeNe explained. "Get it?"

"NeNe, this isn't the Brownies." Dickie went over to the desk again, picking up a back issue of *The Wall Street Journal*. As he thumbed through the pages, looking for ideas, he told the girls. "Let's get serious here now, okay? We need something with class. Like A.T. and T. IBM. Nabisco..."

"I don't think we should go *that* far, Dickie," Bette said. "I mean, we are just kids, after all...."

"There's that bad attitude again," Dickie said. "Look, if you guys don't want to take this serious and put forth...whoah, hold it!"

"What now?" June asked.

Dickie looked over at Bette. "What did you just say a second ago?"

"Out loud or under my breath?" Bette said cynically.

"Never mind," Dickie said, waving her silent. He closed his eyes, concentrating. He looked a little like a dwarf psychic waiting for a call from the beyond.

"I said we're just kids, after all," Bette remembered.

"Yes! That's it!" Dickie said. "Ha ha, it'll be perfect!"

Eleven

"Kidco?" Jim Clark said, looking across his desk at the three children standing before him.

"Yes, sir," Dickie affirmed. "We're a corporation now!"

Clark smiled patiently, then laughed lightly. "Now I see. And my punchline is supposed to be 'You've got to be Kid, Inc.', right?"

"I beg your pardon?" Dickie asked.

"Kid, Inc. Kidding. You've got to be kidding," Clark explained. "This is a joke, isn't it?"

Dickie's sisters fidgeted and looked down at their feet with embarrassment, but Dickie refused to be so easily discouraged. Undaunted, he took another step forward and presented the sales pitch he'd stayed up most of the night concocting.

"We call ourselves Kidco and our specialty is wholesale manure. 'Buy it from us and you won't have to fuss', that's our motto!" As an added inducement, Dickie threw in a knowing wink as he laid out the bottom line. "And we promise not to screw ya royal like Mr. Peterjohn!"

"I see. . . ." Clark nibbled reflectively on the nub of a pencil eraser as he looked past the children at the grounds of the golf course. Dickie took advantage of the pause to glance at his sisters for emotional support. Bette was still staring at her shoes, but June was shaking her head with resignation and NeNe made a slashing gesture across her throat as she contorted her face to indicate her certainty that the deal was dead on its feet.

"Lotta help you three are," Dickie whispered at them with annoyance. "I shoulda come by myself."

"We can leave," June offered.

"You're talking about a mighty big job," Clark interrupted, turning his attention back to Dickie. "We need top dressing for the fairways, compost for the gardens, and every time we cut a street we have to seed all the banks. That's a hell of a lot of fertilizer . . ."

Ecstatic that their offer wasn't being rejected outright, Dickie's spirits perked up immediately and he took still another step toward the desk, a confident sparkle firing his eyes as he boasted, "No problem! With a hundred and seventy-two horses, we got a never-ending supply!"

"Except for Buttercup," NeNe put in, coming to Dickie's aid. "She's been constipated."

Clark smiled again. "As long as it isn't contagious," he said and then chuckled.

"Ha ha!" Dickie laughed with exaggeration, signaling behind his back for his sisters to do the same. They didn't. Dickie brought the laugh under control, telling Clark, "Good joke, sir!"

"If you say so," Clark said, pointing to the leather couch along the wall next to his desk. "Why don't you kids have a seat?"

"Yes, sir!" Dickie turned around and beamed at his sisters, holding a thumb up from his closed fist. NeNe returned the gesture happily as they all sat down. NeNe's legs were too short to reach the floor.

"All right," Clark said, clasping his hands together as he leaned forward on his desk to address the children. "Let's say, for the sake of argument, that your fertilizer's as good as Orville Peterjohn's. . . ."

"It's better!" Dickie said. "Ours is organic."

"Okay, better," Clark conceded. "How are you going to deliver all that . . . product?"

"Everything's explained in our contract." Dickie turned to Bette. "Madame secretary . . ."

"*Executive* secretary," Bette said, standing up and opening the ringbound notebook she'd brought along. She took out two sheets of folded paper and handed them to Clark. "We just drew these up this morning."

"How efficient," Clark said, reaching into his pocket for his reading glasses. Once he'd put them on and unfolded the sheets, he began to read, " 'Official contract between Kidco, Dickie Cessna, President, and San Diego Country Estates. Number One: San Diego Country Estates hereby officially hires Kidco to supply it with homemade fertilizer . . . 'Uh, what's this notation next to that? 'T . . . F . . .'?"

"True or false," Dickie explained.

"True or false," Clark repeated. "I see. Well, we'll have to come back to that one. Now, then . . . 'Number Two: San Diego Country Estates hereby agrees to pay Kidco the cheap sum of four dollars a cubic yard for said fertilizer. T . . . F . . .' "

"True or false again," Dickie said helpfully.

"Thank you," Clark said, smiling blandly. "That will depend on the answer to Number One. Okay . . . 'Number Three: Said sum will be paid: A, in advance; B, most in advance, some at the end of the month; C, some in advance, most at the end of the month; D, None of these.' "

"It's multiple choice," NeNe said.

"We figured you'd want to do some negotiating," Dickie added.

"I've been reading contracts for thirty-five years," Clark told the kids, "and I've never seen one quite like this."

"I *told* them to make some of them essays," June said, "but they're too young."

Going back to the contract, Clark read, " 'Number Four: San Diego Country Estates agrees to: A, give; B, loan; C, rent Kidco a motorized golf cart, for the purpose of helping them finish all deliveries before their bedtime.' "

"You've got a lot of them out there," Dickie said, pointing at the window toward the links.

"That's right," Clark said, "and I get ten dollars every time I rent one out." Trading his pencil for a pen, Clark made his first mark on the contract. "So I think I'll answer 'C, rent' to number four."

The kids had been hoping for either of the first two alternatives, but the fact that he'd even answered the question elevated their hopes. Even June's cynicism began to fade and Clark resumed reading the contract.

"'Number Five: This contract cannot be canceled unless Kidco screws up. . . .'"

"That's your safety clause," Dickie told him.

"Not to mention yours," Clark countered. He set the pages down and ran a hand through his hair, thinking the proposal over. Eight youthful eyes watched his every move, and he finally met their collective gaze, telling them, "I have to admit, you sure as hell have a lot of initiative."

"Thanks!" Dickie and Bette said in unison.

"But let's face it," Clark said, leveling his own bottom line. "You're just a bunch of kids. I can't risk what amounts to a multimillion dollar operation just to—"

"Mr. Clark!" Dickie cried out, jumping to his feet. "When you wanted to build the Country Estates, what if everyone told you, 'You have a lot of initiative, but you're just a grown-up'?"

"That's different," Clark maintained.

"Why!? We can't help how old we are. . . ."

"We're freaks of nature!" NeNe exclaimed.

Dickie gave his sister a chiding glance, then moved over to Clark's desk like a trial attorney approaching the jury stand. Abandoning bravado, he opted for sincerity. "You need a job done, Mr. Clark, and we say we can do it. You can't hate us any worse than Mr. Peterjohn, and we'll do it for you cheaper. Just give us a chance. Please . . ."

Clark sighed and leaned back in his chair. He looked the children over once more, then let his eyes drift to the models and blueprints that filled the office. He seemed lost in thought, and Dickie held back his urge to continue pleading. Stepping back from the desk, he rejoined his sisters. Bette and June were looking at one another worriedly. NeNe had her fingers crossed.

Clark finally sat upright and reached for his phone. As he checked his rolodex for a number and then dialed it, a perverse smile washed across his face. While he waited for an answer on the other end, he pointed to NeNe, signaling her over, asking, "You know what a raspberry is?"

"It's a fruit grown on bramble bushes in polar and—"

"Not that kind of raspberry," Clark said, motioning for NeNe to stand next to him. "The other kind."

"Oh . . . sure." NeNe puckered up and began to stick out her tongue, but Clark held up his hand for her to wait.

"Hello, Orville?" he said into the receiver. "Jim Clark here. Listen I've been thinking over your new price for fertilizer, and I've come to a decision. . . . Yeah, here it is. . . . Listen carefully."

Holding the receiver out to NeNe, Clark nodded, then winked at the other kids while NeNe stuck her tongue out and blew a Bronx cheer that sounded as if it were coming from someone twice her size.

Twelve

Orville Peterjohn yanked the phone away from his ear, letting the sound of NeNe's overripe raspberry spill out into his study.

"What the devil . . . ?" he said, pounding a fist on his desk, a monolithic hulk of polished oak. The rest of the study was equally imposing in its trumped-up grandeur. Orville Peterjohn was obviously a man who liked to surround himself with constant reminders of his wealth.

When the buzz ceased to sound from the phone, Orville brought the receiver back to his ear and barked, "I want an explanation, Clark! What's the meaning of this uncalled—"

A loud click at the other end expressed Clark's sentiments, and Orville found himself arguing with a dial tone.

"Why, the nerve of that bastard!" Orville howled, slamming down the phone. Reaching across the desk, he rammed his finger into one of the buttons on his intercom.

"Sir?" a woman's voice came over the small speaker.

"Get me Jim Clark at the San Diego Country Estates," Orville commanded. "We were disconnected during a call."

"Yes, sir."

Orville rose from his chair and withdrew a thick cigar from the glass humidor on his desk. Fondling the cigar, he strode over to the window and drew back the curtains, staring out at the rolling, landscaped grounds of his estate, taking reassurance from its mere presence. He was still agitated from the phone call, however, and muttered to himself, "Something stinks around here, and I don't like the smell of it."

"Did you say something to me, Dad?" Harvey Peterjohn said as he walked into the office.

Orville whirled around, startled. The cigar went flying from his hand and fell inside an ornamental vase resting on a marble stand next to the window.

"How many times have I warned you about barging into my study without knocking!?" he barked at his son as he reached into the vase. His hand barely fit through the neck of the container, and even when he pushed up the sleeves of his sweater, he couldn't stuff his arm down far enough to grab hold of the cigar. When he tried to pull his hand back out, he found it was stuck. "Now see what you made me do?"

"Gee, I'm sorry, Dad," Harvey said, coming over to lend a hand. As he grabbed the vase and held it firmly in place while his father struggled to tug his hand free, he explained, "Elizabeth told me to tell you that Mr. Clark is in a meeting right now and can't speak to you."

"Oh, is that a fact?" Orville said icily, his face turning red from the strain of his effort. "We'll see about that!"

"Maybe I should go get some oil to pour over your hand," Harvey suggested. "I bet that would help loosen it up."

"You'll pour nothing into this vase, you little dunce!" Orville shouted. "It's an antique. What were you coming in here for in the first place anyway?"

"Well . . . uh . . . I was just wondering if . . . you see, I—"

"Is that any way to talk?" Orville shouted. "How do you expect to get anywhere in the business world if you're going to hem and haw all the time? If you want to be taken serious, know what you want and say what you want. Don't beat around the bush."

"I was hoping you could raise my allowance," Harvey said.

"You what?!!" Orville roared, at the same time jerking

his hand so hard it popped out of the vase, and he staggered a few steps backward. Harvey, still clutching the vase, was thrown off balance and stumbled in the other direction. Slamming into the wall, he dropped the vase and it fell to the tiled floor, shattering loudly into several dozen pieces. He looked down at the mess with horror. Not sure what else to do, he crouched over and picked up the cigar lying amidst the shards, then snapped a loose ceramic sliver off it as he carried it over to his father.

"I said I think you've been paying me too much allowance," Harvey said, handing the cigar to his father. "Can I light that for you, Dad?"

Orville grabbed the cigar from his son's hand and pointed to the door. "Out, you good-for-nothing whippersnapper!"

"I'll pay for the vase, I promise," Harvey said, shrinking away from his father.

"Oh, you'll pay for it, all right!" Orville warned him. "Now get out of my sight before I have you glue it back together, from the inside!"

"Yes, Father."

As Harvey was on his way out the door, Elizabeth's voice came back over the intercom, saying, "Mr. Peterjohn? Howard Carpenter is here to see you. Should I send him in?"

"Carpenter?" Orville growled. "Hell, no, I don't want to see him right now. Tell him to leave whatever . . . No, no, wait!" A glimmer of sudden inspiration came to the man's eyes. "Yes, send him in. Right now! Oh, and after we're done meeting, I want a janitor in here to clean up a little mess my son made."

"It *was* the vase I heard, then," Elizabeth guessed. "Yes, Mr. Peterjohn. I'll see to it. . . ."

By the time Orville had circled around his desk and plopped down into his chair, a tall, dishevelled-looking man in his midthirties swept into the room, wearing a double-breasted jacket that was twenty years out of fashion and a wrinkled red shirt that clashed merrily with his baggy slacks. He was waving a manila envelope in the air as if it were the winning ticket in the Irish Sweepstakes.

"I got 'em!" he told Orville excitedly. "Ho, ho, you aren't going to believe them, I'm telling you!"

"Believe what?" Orville said skeptically. "Are you telling me that you finally got pictures?"

"Yes, yes!" Carpenter said, reaching into the envelope. "I followed your wife all during her trip to San Diego, and yesterday I hit the jackpot. These are taken at the zoo there. This guy . . . look how *old* he is . . . he took her there and, I swear, they were holding hands practically the whole time they were there. And afterward, they went to a cozy—"

"All right, all right!" Orville said, waving the other man silent as he looked over the series of snapshots. He'd only looked at two of them when he let all the pictures drop on the desk, backside up. A fresh burst of anger swelled up inside him, and he tried to keep it under control as he lit his cigar, then blew a thick, noxious cloud into Carpenter's face. "Of course the guy looks *old*, you moron. It's her father!"

"Her what?" Carpenter said between coughs. "Father?"

"Yes, Carpenter. Do you know what a father is?" Orville sneered. "Look, I hired a detective to find out if my wife was committing adultery, not incest!"

"But how was I supposed to know . . .?"

"Because you're *paid* to know, that's why!" Orville raged, flipping over the pictures and pointing at the figures depicted there. "And who taught you how to focus a camera?"

"Well, I had to take them without looking," Carpenter said. "I didn't want them to get suspicious."

Orville shook his head to himself, blowing more smoke. "Why me?" he muttered.

"I'm sorry," Carpenter apologized. "I'll make it up to you."

"I'm glad to hear you say that," Orville said, tapping the tip of his cigar in the ash tray next to him. "I've got something else for you to look into. It's a little less demanding, so I'm sure you might have half a chance of getting results. . . ."

Thirteen

NeNe had always had a streak of tomboy in her, and one of her proudest possessions was a gleaming red, king-size Radio Flyer wagon. Since receiving it for Christmas several years before, she'd put the rugged vehicle to a variety of uses, ranging from a racer in which to ride down the steeper hills near home to a carriage she could hitch up to Buttercup and have herself driven around the neighborhood in grand style. Lest any of the other children, particularly Dickie, be overly tempted to lay claim to the wagon for their own uses, one of the first things she'd done with it had been to take a Magic Marker and boldly write on the side panel PROPERTY OF NENE. Today, however, she was a full-fledged business partner, ready to make her first major sacrifice in the name of the new corporation's greater good. After hosing down the wagon and drying it clean, NeNe had taken a pint of white paint from the garage and was now brushing out her name on the panel. Next to the crossed-out area, she carefully painted KIDCO.

"There!" she said, taking a step back to look at her handiwork. "That's the closest we'll come to a company car right off, I'll bet!"

The sun was pouring down from the afternoon sky, and while she waited for the paint to dry, NeNe cleaned the brush and put the can back in the garage. She was about to leave when she spotted a calendar hanging over her father's workbench. Above the dates was a picture of a showhorse and an advertisement for Ramona Life Insurance and Casualty Company. NeNe stared at the calendar a few seconds, letting an idea gel in her mind. Then, smiling widely, she ran from the garage and grabbed hold of the wagon, dragging it along behind her as she hurried to the equestrian center.

A pickup truck carrying sacks of feed was parked in front of the stables, and Mr. Cessna was talking with the man behind the wheel as NeNe ran up to them.

"Does that cover everything I owe you, Homer?" Mr. Cessna was asking the man as he handed him a check.

Homer compared the figures on the check with those on his bill, nodding his head. "Yup."

"Thanks to Dickie, I'm becoming your best customer these days."

"Yup," Homer said, pocketing the check and handing Mr. Cessna his receipt as he started the pickup.

NeNe looked at the side of the truck, where the words WOODWARD'S FEED STORE were painted on the panels. She compared the work with that she'd done on the wagon, pouting slightly.

"Mr. Woodward?" she asked the driver.

"Yup?" Homer replied, looking down at her.

"How'd you get your lettering on the truck to look so neat?"

"I think he probably had a professional painter do it for him," Mr. Cessna told his daughter. "It's neat because whoever did it used a stencil for the letters."

"Yup," Homer agreed, shifting his truck and waving to the Cessnas as he drove off.

"Shoot," NeNe grumbled, looking back at her paint job. "Now I find out. . . ."

"Oh, darling, I think it looks fine," Mr. Cessna said. "The freehand touch is more in fitting with your image, anyway."

"I guess so. . . ."

"Tell you what," Mr. Cessna said, lifting up one of the huge bags of feed Homer had just dropped off. Setting the bag sideways on the wagon, he continued, "For your first official business trip, how about running this bag into the stable for me? Dickie knows where it goes."

"Sure," NeNe said. She started to pull the wagon away, then stopped and looked back at her father. "Hey, Dad, did you get that calendar in the garage for free or did you pay for it?"

"For free, from my insurance agent," Mr. Cessna explained. "It's his way of seeing to it that I keep thinking about my policy throughout the year."

"Sort of like free advertising, right?" NeNe said.

"Yes, I guess you could say that." Mr. Cessna smiled at his daughter. "You're beginning to sound like Dickie."

"Well, he *is* my brother," NeNe said, hauling her load around to the opened stable doors and then inside.

Dickie was in the first stall, standing on a footstool as he pitched hay down into the trough of one of the older horses.

"Attaboy, Big Red," Dickie encouraged. "Eat up. The more you eat, the more we make. . . ."

Big Red was apparently less enthusiastic about that particular philosophy than Dickie. After taking a few more bites, the steed pulled its head out of the trough and started to back out of its stall.

"Oh, no you don't," Dickie said, nudging Big Red slightly with his pitchfork until the horse reluctantly went back to its feeding. "That's it. A nice full meal, then some exercise and you'll be ready to make a nice, hefty donation to the general fund!"

"Hi, Dickie!" NeNe called out, stopping before the stall. "Dad said you'd know where to put this feed."

"Yeah," Dickie said, giving Big Red an affectionate pat on the hindquarters on his way out of the stall. "It's down at the other end of the stable."

NeNe stepped to one side, letting Dickie take hold of the wagon's handle before asking him, "Well, don't you notice anything different?"

"Huh?"

"About the wagon."

Dickie looked, then broke out smiling. "'Property of Kidco'. Hey, that's great, NeNe! Only next time you ought to use a stencil."

"I was going to," NeNe fibbed, "but I figured doing it this way would go along better with our image."

"Hey, that's a good point, NeNe," Dickie said, wheeling the wagon down the center space between the two rows of stalls. "You're thinking like a vice-president!"

"Thanks, Dickie!" NeNe said brightly. "And I was also thinking maybe we should make up a calendar with our name on it. We could pass it around and people would always be thinking about us."

"Another good idea!" Dickie said. "Of course, I was already thinking along those lines, you understand."

"Oh, of course," NeNe teased.

Bette's voice suddened blared out from one of the stables. "Look out!"

Dickie and NeNe froze, just as a flying clump of manure crash-landed on the clearing in front of them. They traced the flight path to the stall where Bette and June were both hard at work with shovels.

"Hey, what's the big idea?" Dickie said. "You trying to assassinate me or something?"

"'Kidco President Killed by Flying Turd!'" Bette joked.

"Very funny," Dickie said. "Hey, June, you don't look so happy."

Dickie's oldest sister looked up from her shoveling and

said, "What do you expect? You think maybe I'd be doing this while I sang 'Whistle While You Work?'"

"That's not such a bad idea," Dickie said. "If you don't want to do that, just think that what you're doing is going to turn into money in your pocket before you know it."

June shook her head miserably as she went back to her task, clearing out the last few shovelfuls of manure as she whined, "Phyllis works at McDonald's; Christine sells clothes in a boutique; Sally just has to type letters in her father's office—all my friends do *normal* things to earn a living. Me, I have a job where I end up smelling like a horse . . . no, even worse. I end up smelling like a horse's—"

"June, June, June," Dickie interrupted, waving his arms. "Please, there are children here."

"Well, I'm done for the day!" June said, propping her shovel against the stall and walking out of the stables.

"She'll be okay," Bette said, helping Dickie and NeNe unload the feed sack in the back corner. "It's just that we've all been working so hard on this the past few days."

"Yeah," Dickie said. "It's always rough that first week, they say. But once we get our first check things'll be different, you can count on it."

The threesome went out the back door of the stables to look at their collected pile of straw and drying manure. It was higher than any of them ever remembered seeing it.

"The Mount Everest of poop," Dickie said proudly. "All we gotta do is let it compost, then break it down, and we'll have our first load of bonafide Kidco fertilizer. I can hardly wait!"

"Maybe we should take a picture of it," NeNe suggested. "For the calendar . . ."

"Are you kidding?" Dickie said. "You think anyone's going to want to look at a heap of horse manure every time they check to see what day it is?"

"Dickie's right, NeNe," Bette said. "Forget pictures. What's this about a calendar, though?"

NeNe and Dickie got into an argument claiming responsibility for the idea as the three of them went around the stables and headed back to the house. Halfway there, they caught up with June, who was having her own argument with Frank in front of his car.

"Frank," June said with an air of desperate finality. "I've

been shoveling shit all afternoon, and I've got an English paper to write for Monday. I'm too *tired* to go out tonight...."

"Cripe, June, you haven't been the same since you started working," Frank complained.

June leaned forward, no longer interested in whether or not her boyfriend smelled the equestrian aroma clinging to her clothing. "Well, if you weren't always broke, Frank, I wouldn't *have* to work!"

"June..." Frank said, following her away from his car toward the house.

"Leave me alone, you freeloader!" June snapped over her shoulder.

Stung by the insult, Frank stopped and watched June storm up the front steps and vanish inside, slamming the door behind her. He turned around and kicked the ground angrily as he headed back to his car. Dickie broke away from NeNe and Bette, catching up with Frank as he was starting his car.

"Hey, Frank," he said jovially. "Just thought I'd give you an update on that loan. Let's see, a ten dollar loan, plus two dollars' interest, plus fifty cents a day late payment penalty—"

"Screw off, Dickie!" Frank said, stepping on the accelerator and screeching off down the road.

As NeNe and Bette came up beside him, Dickie watched the retreating automobile, shaking his head sadly. "Boy, I sure hope I don't end up having to repossess his car."

"Poor Frank," Bette said. "Maybe we should offer him a job."

"No way," Dickie said firmly. "We're family-owned and family-operated and we're going to keep it that way...at least until we're big enough to start franchises!"

"Franchises?" NeNe wondered aloud. "Like McDonald's?"

"Sure, why not?" Dickie shrugged. "The sky's the limit if you're willing to work for it!"

"I think we should take it just a step at a time," Bette advised. "I mean, we still haven't made any money yet."

"That's gonna change real soon," Dickie said, raising a defiant fist in the air. "Today, Ramona! Tomorrow, the world!"

Bette looked at her sister dubiously. "I think Dickie's been smelling too much manure...."

Fourteen

Bette nearly started a small-scale family feud the following morning, spending so much time in the shower that there was hardly any hot water left for the others. But she was still feeling paranoid about any lingering traces of telltale odor from her shoveling stint over the weekend, so when she went to her room to dress, she bombarded herself with a layer of baby powder, then splashed on enough perfume to ward off, if not kill, any of the flies that had been her constant companions in the stables. As a finishing touch, she mulled over her wardrobe for ten minutes trying to decide what to wear before finally settling on her Easter dress from the previous spring. By the time she had finished dressing, she was so used to the smell of the perfume that she wondered if it was a sufficient dose to attract the right kind of attention. Deciding to be on the safe side, she poured out another palmful and then rubbed her hands together before spreading the scent all over her.

"There!" she said when she was finished. After looking in the mirror long enough to brush her hair one hundred and seventeen times, she left her room and bounded down the stairs to the kitchen, where the other children were quickly finishing their breakfast.

"Well, if it isn't the Shower Queen of... wheeeeeeeew!" Catching a whiff of Bette's perfume as she walked past the table, Dickie clutched at his throat and began making gagging noises. He slid from his chair to the kitchen floor, pretending to be going into death throes. "I... I... I'm a g... g... goner," he gasped, pointing a shaking finger at Bette. "Biochemical warfare!"

"Cut it out, Dickie," Bette said, opening the refrigerator and taking out a pitcher of fresh juice. "You're not being funny."

"Bette, honey," Mrs. Cessna said, wincing as she came

over to her daughter. "You *do* smell like you're wearing just a touch too much perfume."

NeNe sniffed and made a face as she pushed her unfinished cereal away. "I'm suddenly not hungry any more. . . ."

Dickie got to his feet and suggested to NeNe, "Let's go out to the stables, where the air is fresh!"

"Okay, okay, I can take a hint," Bette said as soon as she finished her juice. "I'm leaving! I'll ride my bike so I air out. So what if I ruin my good dress! At least you—"

"Bette, I'll give you a ride to school, don't worry," Mrs. Cessna said. "What's the special occasion, though?"

"What's the matter, can't I look nice?" Bette asked hostilely.

Dickie informed his mother, "Bette's giving an interview to Neil Brody about Kidco during lunch period, that's why she's all spiffed up."

"That's not true!" Bette said. Rushing over to her brother, she whispered, "You said you weren't going to tell!"

"Sorry," Dickie said, crumbling to his knees and beginning to gag again. "It m . . . m . . . must have been the f . . . f . . . fumes."

"Honestly," Bette said, leaving the kitchen. "Mother, I'll be waiting in the car."

"I'll ride my bike today," NeNe said, getting up from the table.

"Me too," Dickie said.

June, who'd kept quiet all this time while she tried to study for her test, reached over to the counter for the phone and said, "I'm giving Frank a call and seeing if he can take me to school."

"Thanks a lot for nothing, you guys!" Bette shouted on her way out the door. "I ought to tell Neil that you're all a bunch of inconsiderate jerks!"

"Hey, just a second now!" Dickie said, jumping to his feet and running out the door after Bette.

"Don't say a word to me, Dickie Cessna!" Bette warned, hearing her brother approaching from behind as she headed for the car.

"Oh, come on, Sis!" Dickie said. "I was just giving you a hard time to get even for you using all the hot water this morning, that's all."

"I don't want to hear it!"

"You look real nice, Bette," Dickie said, laying on the charm. "I mean it."

"Ha!"

"No, really. If I know Neil, he won't be able to help but take notice when you're talking to him today."

Bette opened the passenger door and got into the car, obviously placated by Dickie's flattery. "I sure hope you're right, Dickie."

"Trust me," Dickie said. "I know how us guys think. Ol' Neil's going to go for you in a big way, especially if you give him a good story about how neat Kidco is."

"Don't worry," Bette assured Dickie. "I wouldn't tell him you're a jerk. I was just upset, that's all."

"Well, that sure is a relief!" Dickie said. As Mrs. Cessna came out and got in behind the wheel of the family car, Dickie leaned forward and offered Bette one last piece of advice. "To be on the safe side, you might want to ride to school with the window down. Know what I mean?"

"Hey, I'm an executive secretary," Bette reminded him. "I can handle myself." Looking over at Mrs. Cessna, she said, "Mom, could you roll down your window a ways, too?"

Slapping the hood, Dickie stepped back from the car and waved. "Good luck, Bette!"

"Thanks, I'll need it," Bette said.

All the way to school and through her first three classes, Bette's mind was tied with knots of expectation over her pending interview with Neil Brody, and when it came time to go to the cafeteria to meet with him over lunch, she almost ran to the girls' room to hide in one of the stalls. Her nerve stayed with her, though, and finally the moment of truth arrived.

Neil was thirteen and he looked every bit the editor of the school paper. Tall and thin, he had a full head of sandy hair and thick glasses that gave him an owlish, academic appearance. He was sitting at one of the small tables along the cafeteria wall, alone. When Bette came over, he promptly stood up and gestured to one of the other chairs, saying, "Have a seat, Bette."

"Yes, thank you," Bette said nervously, sitting down.

Neil opened the notebook in front of him and looked over the scribbled handwriting filling the page as he said, "Now, I've already been briefed on a lot of background from

Dickie," Neil said, overly mature. "I just have a few questions to round things out."

"You already talked to Dickie?" Bette asked, feeling both anger and disillusionment.

"Well, he sits across from me in history class second period," Neil said. "Our teacher was sick and our substitute gave us a study period, so I mostly spent the time talking to Dickie. I didn't want to have to hog your whole lunch period."

"But, I . . . you aren't hogging anything!" Bette said. "I have all the time in the world! But can you first tell me, was it Dickie's idea to fill you in first on our company?"

"Oh, no, that was my doing," Neil said, smiling with professional pride. "A good reporter always checks two sources to make sure he's got his facts straight."

"I see. . . . Well, ask away!" Bette said, shifting uncomfortably in her seat. She knew that her perfume had faded considerably, but she wondered if any of the scent remained. Neil seemed to be all business. He asked her a dozen or so questions about Kidco, how they operated, what plans they had for the future, and so on, seldom looking up from his notebook as he wrote down Bette's responses. Bette watched him longingly, waiting for him to take notice of her the way Dickie'd said he would.

"Does being in Kidco take up all your time on the weekends?" Neil asked, still staring down at his wretched handwriting.

"Not all of it," Bette said, leaning forward slightly, trying to sneak into Neil's field of vision. "Dickie and NeNe have the first shift on Saturday. That means I'm free Saturday afternoons . . . Neil."

"Mmmmmmm, yes," Neil murmured, writing it all down. If he detected the urgency in Bette's voice, he didn't show it. "Go on. . . ."

"For example," Bette went on, letting her hands drift slowly across the table top toward Neil. "If *someone* wanted to take me to the Saturday matinee at the Ramona, I'd be able to go. . . . I'd be delighted to go, in fact. . . ."

The bell on the wall over their heads suddenly clanged into life, and both kids jumped in place with surprise. Then Neil closed his notebook and stood up. "Well, it looks like we ended up talking longer than I'd planned. I guess that'll do it, though."

"We could talk more after school!" Bette suggested, leaping to her feet.

"That's okay," Neil said, acknowledging her with a brief glance. "I think I have enough for a story. Thanks, Bette."

"Yeah," Bette said, her spirits sinking. "Sure . . . my pleasure."

"See ya around. . . ."

Bette waited until Neil had left the cafeteria, then sniffed back the tears she'd been holding in check at the corners of her eyes.

Fifteen

Howard Carpenter had tried all week to come up with some concrete answers as to why Jim Clark had terminated Orville Peterjohn's services as provider of fertilizer for the San Diego Country Estates. Clark wasn't talking, though, and nobody else Carpenter had tried to speak with had given him any worthwhile information either. He didn't even have any clue about who was replacing Peterjohn as Clark's client. Knowing full well that Orville was expecting a progress report any day now, the private detective decided that it was time he resorted to more diabolical means of doing business.

That afternoon, he appeared at the golf course in a tweed suit, with a clipboard and a phony set of documents that said he was an inspector for the County Health Department. Bypassing the clubhouse, he made his way directly toward the building used by the groundskeepers to store their equipment and other materials used for maintaining the links. The door to the office was open, so he walked in, presenting his credentials to the head groundskeeper, a crotchety, thick-chested man who wore a patch on his coveralls that said his name was Earl.

"Health Department, huh?" Earl said, looking up from the clipboard, then handing it back to Carpenter.

"That is correct, sir," Carpenter replied.

"Well, this sure as hell ain't the kitchens, mac," Earl told him. "Only food you can inspect here is in my lunch bucket, and I can already assure you my wife's cooking is so bad no disease worth its salt would bother hanging around any food she gets her hands on."

Carpenter chuckled for an appropriate length of time, then tapped a pen on the edge of the clipboard, saying, "Well, I'm not here to inspect either the kitchens or the foodstuffs, but rather your storage rooms for seed, weedkiller, fertilizer, insecticide, and . . . oh, yes, and fertilizer."

"You already said that once," Earl said. "What do you gotta see all that crap for?"

"It's my job," Carpenter said succinctly.

Earl broke out laughing as he went out of the office, taking a pipe from his coveralls and putting it between his teeth.

"I fail to see the humor," Carpenter said stuffily.

"You said something about fertilizer, then I said something about crap, then you said something about your job. Fertilizer, crap, job. Get it? Oh, shit, that's a riot!" Earl stopped walking suddenly and began howling with mirth all over. "Shit! That's still another one! Oh, man, too much!"

Carpenter looked at Earl strangely as they entered the main storage room. "Perhaps I should inspect your pipe before anything else," he said matter-of-factly. "What exactly is it you smoke in that thing?"

Earl's eyes narrowed into venemous slits. He stopped laughing and lit his pipe, then blew smoke in Carpenter's face, taunting, "You tell me, wise guy!"

"Look, I'm sorry. Excuse me," Carpenter said, changing both his tone and tack, trying to salvage his visit. "That was rude of me."

"Well, now, that's what I like to hear," Earl said, puffing away contentedly on the pipe now. He waved one hand to take in the entire storage room, which was filled with stacked sacks of grass seed, canisters of various sprays, riding lawnmowers, sprinkler assemblies and a variety of tools and other pieces of equipment. "Here's what makes us tick. What's a guy like you look for here, being from the Health Department and all? You looking to see if we got rats or something, because we got no problems—"

"This is merely a routine inspection," Carpenter said,

making a beeline for the cinderblock wall where bags of fertilizer were stacked. Only a few bags remained, and they all had the Peterjohn name on them. "Ah, I see you stock this line of fertilizer products. Good firm, Peterjohn. We've never had problems with them."

"Good for you," Earl said. "We never had problems with them, either, until old man Peterjohn got greedy and upped his price. Now we say to hell with the bastard! Who needs him, anyway?"

"Mmmmmmm, yes. I see your point," Carpenter said, making note of Earl's comments for his own future reference. "But who is it you're doing business with on that front now, Earl... do you mind if I call you Earl?"

"It's my name...."

"Yes, of course," Carpenter said, beginning to sweat inside his suit. "As I was saying, we have to know who will be supplying you with fertilizer, so that we can inspect their plant and make sure that their packaging is up to industry standards and what not...."

"Well, as a matter of fact, we just switched over to a new firm, and they're due any moment with our first shipment," Earl said. "Outfit by the name of Kidco...."

"Kidco?" Carpenter said, jotting the information down and trying to remain casual. "How do you spell that?"

"It's short for Kid Company or Kid Corporation or something like that," Earl said. "Weird, huh? Must have something to do with goats, I guess...."

"Then you've never met these people before?"

Earl shook his head, taking a last puff of his pipe before tapping the ash out into an old distributor cap being used for an ash tray. "Nope. Boss hired them himself, so they must be pros, that's all I can say."

Just then there was a knock on the rolling garage door across the room from where the men were standing. As he went to answer it, Earl told Carpenter, "That must be them now. Funny, I didn't hear any truck pull up...."

Trying to contain his excitement at having stumbled upon the solution to his assignment, Carpenter strode to the door as Earl was pulling it open. Both men were dumbfounded at the sight that awaited them.

NeNe was standing before the doorway, wearing an oversized army surplus gas mask. Tilting her head upward, she squinted at Earl through the scratched, smoky glass of the mask's goggles, then turned slightly and gestured behind her, where Dickie, also wearing a gas mask, was driving one of the club's motorized golf carts toward the building, dragging behind him the red Kidco wagon, which was piled high with fine, black compost.

Earl gaped numbly at the two kids, who looked more like mutant insects than true children with their masks, then slowly looked over at Carpenter, muttering, "I think maybe you oughta take pictures if you're going to report this, pal. Nobody's going to believe it if you just write it down."

"I don't even think I'll do that," Carpenter said, still looking at the children. NeNe waved at him politely, and when Dickie drove by on his way to deliver the compost, he looked up at the detective and said, in a voice that was muffled by the mask, "Hi!"

As he walked past Earl on his way out of the storage room, Carpenter said, "I think I'm going to need that camera after all. I'll be right back."

Sixteen

There were no model cars in Dickie's bedroom. No posters of cover girls or sports figures or rock and roll idols. No hidden copies of *Playboy*. No packs of cigarettes. No comic books. No exercise equipment guaranteed to change him from a ninety-eight pound weakling into the guys girls gush at on the beach. No, Dickie Cessna chose to surround himself instead with entrepreneurial paraphernalia, the stuff of big business. There were placards and logos of big corporations set about like shrines, and the posters on the wall depicted the likes of Howard Hughes, Nelson Rockefeller, and Uncle Scrooge McDuck. The tickertape machine next to his desk was only an imitation; the back issues of *Fortune* magazine were the real things. The most recent addition to this fiscal grotto was the framed copy of Kidco's first contract with the San Diego Country Estates, hanging prominently over Dickie's desk.

Dickie was sitting up in bed, writing with a frenzy on the legal pad propped on his lap, when there came a knock on his door.

"Yeah?"

Mr. Cessna opened the door and came into the room. "It's after ten, son. Time to put away your homework. . . ."

"I finished that a long time ago," Dickie said. "These are papers of incorporation for Kidco."

"Is that a fact?"

"Yeah, we have to be official about these things."

"Dickie," Mr. Cessna said, sitting down on the edge of the bed to face his son. "You know I'm proud of you and your sisters for starting your own business, but . . ."

Dickie put down his pen and looked at his father, perplexed. "But what, Dad?"

"Well . . ." Mr. Cessna said, pausing while he tried to choose a tactful course. "Do you know what an obsession is, Dickie?"

"Sure. It's like when a guy looks up girls' dresses."

Mr. Cessna flinched slightly and felt his ears flush red as he smiled awkwardly. "That's one kind of obsession," he admitted. "But there're other kinds, too. You see, an obsession means you get so wrapped up in one thing that you forget all the other things that are important in your life. Now, I wouldn't want to see that happen with you and Kidco. Would you?"

Dickie had to think about that for a moment. "I guess not, Pop."

"Good," Mr. Cessna said, relieved. "Okay, now I think those papers can wait until tomorrow. Let's hear your prayers."

Dickie reluctantly set aside the legal pad, sighing. "There's never enough hours in the day." Lying back in bed, he turned his eyes to the ceiling and recited a quick prayer to the light fixture.

> Now I lay me down to sleep,
> And pray the Lord my soul to keep;
> And if I die before I wake,
> I pray the Lord my soul to take. . . .
> And NeNe, Bette and June can split
> My share of the business. . . .

Mr. Cessna eyed his son dubiously, wondering how much he'd taken their little talk to heart. Not wishing to belabor his point, however, he leaned forward to kiss Dickie goodnight, then stood up and headed out of the room, whispering over his shoulder, "Sleep well, son."

"You too, Dad."

After closing the door behind him, Mr. Cessna lingered a moment outside Dickie's room. Moments later, he heard the dull snap of a light switch and the rustling of pages on the other side of the door.

"My son, the workaholic," he mumbled quietly to himself as he moved down the hallway to check on the other children. Bette and NeNe were slumbering soundly in their bunkbeds when he poked his head inside their room. He padded quietly across the carpet and gave each of them a light peck on the cheek, then left the room to retire for the night.

Soon after her father had gone, NeNe slowly opened her eyes. She lay still a while longer, letting herself get used to the dark, then stealthily climbed down from the top bunk, taking care not to wake her sister. After sticking her feet into a pair of slippers, she threw on her bathrobe and silently left the room.

All the lights were out in the house, so she reached out carefully for the railing as she headed down the stairs. Going into the kitchen, she flashed on the light and hurried to one of the cupboards, where she took out a box of brown sugar. She clutched it to her side as she went to the kitchen door and eased open the deadbolt, then slowly turned the doorknob to let herself outside.

It was a clear night, with a nearly full moon throwing down a soft glow on the yard as NeNe circled around to the front flower beds. Peering intently, she spotted the gopher trap her father had set most recently. There were a few stray twigs on the lawn, and she used one of them to tap at the trap until it sprang shut with a loud snap and jumped a few inches into the air.

NeNe's eyes glanced up at the windows of her parents' bedroom as she sucked in her breath, ready to make a mad dash around the house. No lights went on inside the house, though, and she stayed where she was, cautiously removing the trap from the vicinity of the hole. Then, after licking her fingers, she dipped them into the box of brown sugar. Brown crystals clung to her fingertips when she pulled the fingers out and dangled them invitingly above the hole in the flower bed.

"Goofer! Goofer!" she whispered, staring at the orifice. When there was no response from the subterranean dweller, she raised her voice slightly and repeated, "Goofer! Time for your bedtime snack!"

There was a slight stirring near the mouth of the hole, then a small, furry head poked forth, bobbing nervously before the outstretched fingers.

"Attaboy, Goofer!" NeNe said warmly as the gopher emerged from its lair far enough to begin licking at the brown sugar on NeNe's fingertips.

Seventeen

The days advanced and the children increased the efficiency with which they made their work in the stables a part of their daily routine. Their output of fertilizer earmarked for Country Estates grew proportionately, but as the month was drawing to a close, it was clear that the productivity of the horses was surpassing that of Kidco. Instead of diminishing, the composting piles of manure were steadily growing in size. This fact was not lost on Dickie, and as he accompanied his sisters on their last delivery of the month, he was in somber spirits.

"Hey, Dickie, cheer up!" NeNe told him as they headed across the parking lot from the maintenance building to Mr. Clark's office. "This is the big day! Payoff!"

"Yeah!" Bette said bubblingly.

Even June was elated at the prospects before them. "I mean, we must have delivered enough horseshit here to make close to a hundred bucks, don't you think, Dickie?"

Dickie forced a smirk. "Yeah, something like that."

"Have you figured out how much exactly?" Bette asked.

"Of course I have!" Dickie said as they started up the steps leading into the lodge. "I'm the president, aren't I?"

"Well, how much is it?" NeNe asked.

Before Dickie could answer, they entered the reception area outside Mr. Clark's office and Florence greeted them with a broad smile, saying, "Good afternoon, children. You're just in time. Mr. Clark's just writing out a check for you. Why don't you go on in? He's expecting you. . . ."

"Thank you, Florence," Dickie intoned officiously as he strode to the door and held it open for his sisters. As they filed past, NeNe shivered slightly with excitement.

"Don't tell me how much!" she told Dickie. "I want it to be a surprise. . . . It's almost a hundred dollars, right?"

Dickie didn't answer. He followed the others into the room and greeted Clark with a slight wave. "Afternoon, Mr. C."

"Good afternoon, Dickie . . . girls," Clark said, nodding at the children. He finished scrawling his signature on a check, then gingerly ripped it clear of his business ledger. "Now, according to my entries, you delivered one hundred and ninety-six cubic yards of manure. . . ."

"Exactly," Dickie said, referring to the slip of paper he'd taken out of his shirt pocket. "And we paid for rental on the carts up front each time we used them."

"That's correct. So, at four dollars a yard, that comes to . . ." Clark paused dramatically as he handed the check to Dickie, then said, "seven hundred and eighty-four dollars!"

"Whaaaaaa?" June gasped. NeNe and Bette were stunned beyond words as they stared at the check in awe.

"Good first month," Dickie said casually.

"Keep up the good work," Clark told them. "I'm using it up as fast as you're getting it to me."

"You bet!" NeNe said, edging over to her brother's side to gape at the figures on the check.

"Well, we like to have satisfied customers," Dickie said, heading for the door. "We'll let you get back to your work."

Clark grinned at the kids and told them, "If you run into Orville Peterjohn, be sure to rub it in for me, okay?"

"You can count on it," Dickie assured him.

Once the four children were out in the hallway, June grabbed the check from Dickie's hand and started passing it around as she shrieked, "Oh, this is incredible! The dresses I'll be able to buy. . . ."

"Wait until Neil sees me in a permanent," Bette said.

"I'm gonna buy some solid gold roller skates!" NeNe exclaimed!

"Whoah!" Dickie said, stopping at the end of the hallway and grabbing the check from NeNe. He looked at his sisters reproachfully, then lowered the boom. "We're running a business here. This money goes back into the company."

"Dickie!" Bette groaned, sagging visibly. "No!"

"Hey, what kind of a rip-off are you trying to pull?" June demanded.

"What about my roller skates?" NeNe wanted to know.

"Look," Dickie said firmly. "We have to expand our operations here! We got a lotta growth potential to realize!"

"Talk English, Dickie," NeNe said.

"We need more wagons and shovels," Dickie said, beginning to rattle off the possibilities. "We want to establish credit, we gotta take out advertising . . ."

"Advertising?" June said. "What do we need advertising for?"

"To reach the marketplace, that's why!" Dickie looked at NeNe. "Remember your idea about the calendars?"

"I thought it was *your* idea," NeNe said sarcastically, pouting.

"Whatever. Well, that takes money, too." As they headed outside, Dickie went on. "We have to remember the cardinal rule of business. You gotta spend money to make money!"

"Why bother if we never get to spend any on ourselves?" June protested. "I veto your plan, Dickie."

"Me too!" Bette said.

"Me three!" NeNe pitched in. "If I can't get some of the money to spend on what I want, I'm gonna go off and get a paper route or something. . . ."

"Hey, come on, you guys!" Dickie pleaded. "This is the way it's done!"

"What's done is my share of the business, then," Bette warned. "I'll retire, too!"

"Yeah," June joined in on the second offensive. "You can run the whole business yourself, Dickie! How'd you like that?"

"Okay, okay," Dickie relented, trying to stem the mutiny.

"How about if we let everybody take out ten bucks from this as their salary for the month?"

"Cheapskate!" Bette said.

"That comes to forty bucks!" Dickie said. "That's about five percent of our gross income."

"Only ten dollars a month is what's gross," June insisted.

"Yeah," Bette added. "I was thinking more like fifty!"

"Fifty!" Dickie cried out like a wounded man.

"Okay, we'll compromise," NeNe said. "Twenty-five. That makes an even hundred."

"Very good, NeNe," Bette said. "I second that idea."

"I third it," June said.

"You're outnumbered, Dickie," NeNe teased.

Dickie stared at the check longingly, then slowly nodded his head. "Okay, you guys win. But I'm gonna save up my share. As soon as we get big enough to start selling stock, I'm gonna make sure and buy fifty-one percent..."

Eighteen

It took two days for Dickie to arrange for radio and newspaper advertisements touting Kidco and the availability of fresh fertilizer at special introductory rates. It didn't take half as long for the ads to produce results. The day after the ads had appeared, Mr. and Mrs. Cessna were awakened during the early hours of Sunday morning by a sporadic chorus of honking horns.

"Huh?" Mr. Cessna said drowsily, sitting upright in bed and scratching his head as he tried to make sense of the outburst. "What's going on here?"

"If we weren't out in the middle of the country on a Sunday morning, I'd say there's a traffic jam," Mrs. Cessna said as she slipped her arms into her bathrobe and joined her husband at the window overlooking the front yard.

"Give me a pinch to see if I'm dreaming," he said once he pulled open the shade and stared outside. "This can't be happening!"

Oaktree Lane was choked with trucks of all shapes and sizes. There were pickups, dump trucks, a few six- and eight-wheelers, and even a few station wagons, all empty except for their drivers and helpers. As they reached the driveway leading to the nearby stables, the trucks turned in, continuing to give short blasts of their horns to announce their arrival.

"Who . . . who are they?" Mrs. Cessna asked, somewhat fearfully as she clung to her husband's arm.

"I don't know, but I sure as heck aim to find out!"

The door to their bedroom suddenly burst open and Dickie rushed to the window, still in his pajamas. Looking out, he smiled as if it were Christmas.

"Do you know something about this?" Mr. Cessna said. "As if I had to ask."

"They're customers!" Dickie said, turning from the window and racing back out of the bedroom. "Read the paper! Listen to the radio! It's the power of advertising!"

As Dickie bounded up the stairs, shouting for his sisters to wake up and give him a hand, Mr. Cessna turned to his wife and said, "I think we've created a monster."

"Let's go fix them breakfast," Mrs. Cessna said, putting on her slippers. "If we're nice to them, maybe they'll increase our allowance."

But the kids were in too much of a hurry to eat. They were still dressing as they scrambled down the steps and hurried for the front door.

"You guys want some help?" Mr. Cessna offered.

"Naw, we can handle it!" Dickie said, opening the door.

June told her parents, "If we need you, we'll let you know."

"How nice," Mrs. Cessna said dryly, holding back a smile until the children were all out the door. Then she looked at her husband and cracked, "When I was a kid, our idea of being ambitious was to go around shoveling sidewalks during the winter. It looks like times have changed."

"Well, it doesn't snow much down here," Mr. Cessna said, going over to the picture window to watch his offspring greet the truck drivers, pointing to the manure piles behind the stables. "One thing hasn't changed, though. They're still shoveling. . . ."

And shovel they did. From nine in the morning until

midafternoon, the children worked nonstop trying to keep up with the influx of buyers lured by the Kidco advertisements. Some of the drivers, who were mostly farmers, bartered for reduced rates by offering to load their own trucks, and Dickie reluctantly agreed so that he and his sisters could take breaks in shifts and be able to man the cashbox, which filled with the steady stream of payments. The pile of accumulated compost dwindled gradually, until finally there was only a small mound of the fine black substance left to be loaded into the back of the last farmer's truck.

Dickie and Bette shoveled up the fertilizer, and NeNe raked it out so that it filled the truckbed evenly. The farmer, an old man with gnarled, arthritic fingers, watched them work with wondering admiration, then strode over to the card table where June was minding the coffers.

"I gotta admit, I didn't expect a bunch of kids to be running this thing," he said as he pulled out his wallet.

"That's why we call ourselves Kidco," June said pleasantly.

"Good point."

June punched a few buttons on her pocket calculator, then said, "We figure you for eight cubic yards, so that comes to thirty-two dollars. Trim ten percent off that as our introductory special and you owe us twenty-eight dollars and eighty cents."

"Here's thirty," the farmer said, handing her three tens. "Keep the change."

"Thank you," June said, taking care to slip the bills into the cashbox without letting him see the contents.

"Thank *you*," the farmer replied. "It's worth a tip and takin' a little drive to save as much money as I did today. See you next week?"

"Let's make it *two* weeks," Dickie said, walking stiffly as he came over to the table. "We have to give the horses time to do their best work, and to let the piles compost."

"Of course, I understand. Good day to you now." The farmer doffed his cap to the girls, then climbed into his truck and drove off.

The kids waited until the truck was out of the driveway, then looked at each other, forgetting about their fatigue as they let out excited whoops and jumped up and down with joy.

"What a day!" Dickie beamed. "How'd we do, June!? How'd we do!"

"See for yourself!" June said, throwing open the lid of the cashbox. It was so filled with money that bills spilled out onto the table.

"A killing! We made a killing!" NeNe howled.

"I'll say!" Dickie enthused, clutching a fistful of dollars. "And it's only the beginning!"

June sorted through the bills for a twenty, then held it up and proclaimed, "I say we all deserve a bonus!"

"Hold it!" Dickie said, suddenly serious. But he was too late.

"All those in favor..." June said, raising her hand.

NeNe and Bette both reached for the sky.

"Motion passed!" June handed everyone a twenty, then told Dickie. "Oh, come on, don't be such a stick-in-the-mud. We practically made as much today as we did all last month! Don't start being such a tightwad."

"A good businessman just doesn't get carried away by any windfall profits, that's all," Dickie said, putting his twenty back into the coinbox. "It can be feast one day and famine the next, you know...."

"It's not like we *have* to make *any* money," Bette reminded Dickie. "Come on, be a sport."

NeNe took Dickie's twenty and handed it back to him, saying, "Yeah, Dickie. All work and no play makes... I forget what it makes, but you're supposed to do both, I know that much."

"Well, okay," Dickie said grudgingly, pocketing the bill.

"Look, someone else," Bette said, pointing toward the main road, where a sports car was slowing down as it neared the driveway.

"I'll go tell him we're out of stock," Dickie said, moving away from the others. "I don't know where he expected to put any fertilizer anyway."

"I saw that car drive by a couple times before," June remembered.

As Dickie approached the driveway and signaled for the car to stop, its driver pushed the accelerator and drove off down the road, picking up speed.

"Hey, that was the guy from the Health Department we met that day we made our first delivery to the golf course,"

Dickie told the girls as he returned to the table. "I wonder what he wanted."

"Maybe he thought we were selling horse pies," June joked.

Nineteen

The day Howard Carpenter's report on the Kidco fertilizer operation arrived with the morning mail, Orville Peterjohn was in a foul mood. A bout of indigestion had woken him in the middle of the night, disrupting a dream in which he'd been on the verge of having his face pictured on the cover of *Time* magazine as its Man of the Year. He hadn't been able to get back to sleep, and the time he'd spent reading through his company ledgers dealing with last month's business had aggravated his ulcer to the point where he was longing for the indigestion. When he came upon Carpenter's report while he was finishing his breakfast in the study, Orville felt his hopes rise perceptibly.

"Ah, this should help set the day right," he muttered to himself, swallowing the last bite of toast as he opened the envelope and pulled out the report. Before reading anything, he paused long enough to pluck a cigar from his humidor and light it.

His first puffs were contented ones, but as he read the report, he began seething with fury, burning down the cigar like a short fuse.

"Outrage! It's a royal outrage!" he fumed, setting down the report long enough to grab the phone and dial Carpenter's number. The detective answered on the seventh ring, sounding as if he were only half-awake.

"Hullo?"

"What's the matter with you, Carpenter? Damn it, man, it's almost nine o'clock!"

"Night or day?"

"What do you mean, night or . . . oh, I get it. You were

out having a good time on the money I paid you for this piece of shit report I'm now holding in my hands, is that it?"

"Oh, no, sir," Carpenter said. Orville could hear him stifle a yawn before adding, "I was out doing some surveillance."

"Surveillance at the singles bars, unless I miss my guess."

"What are you calling about, Mr. Peterjohn? It should all be in the report."

"If those little snots' heads were on a silver platter in the report it might be what I was looking for," Orville grumbled. "As it turns out, though, all I get from you is a bunch of facts about this Kidco crap those Cessna whelps are peddling. Damn it, Carpenter, I hired you to produce results, not a damn newspaper feature story! Carpenter, I'm losing farmers who've been buying from me for twenty years!"

"I know it's a tough break, sir, but from what I've looked into, there's really nothing you can do about those—"

"Oh, yeah?" Orville interrupted, blowing smoke into the mouthpiece. "I'll tell you *one* thing I *can* do about it; I can bounce a bumbling detective who can't take care of four little brats peddling homemade horseshit! You're fired!"

"But, sir..."

"Fired!"

Orville slammed down the phone and angrily tapped an inch of ash from the end of his cigar as he tossed the report into the wastebasket. When he put the cigar back in his mouth, it worked like a pacifier, venting a portion of his hostility in small bursts of smoke. He recounted his encounter with two of the Cessna children in Jim Clark's office the week before last, and the idea that those young upstarts were responsible for a fourteen percent drop in his business just in the past week was contemptible. There had to be something he could do, and it didn't take long for him to strike upon the most obvious course of action.

Leaning across his desk, Orville poked one of the buttons on the intercom and bellowed, "Harvey! I want to see you in my study."

After a slight pause, Harvey's voice came over the small speaker. "I'm in the bathroom, Dad. I'll be right—"

"Now!"

Harvey was familiar enough with that tone of voice to know that his father meant it. The sound of a flushing toilet was still sounding over the intercom when Harvey blundered into the study, fumbling at his zipper. Reaching Orville's desk, he stood upright and might have even saluted if he thought he could do it without his pants dropping.

"Yeah, Dad?"

"Harvey," Orville said, swinging back in his chair. "I want you to arrange something for me . . . a little something to make up for that unfortunate accident with the vase. . . ."

From the look in his father's eyes, Harvey could tell that he wasn't going to care much for the "little something." After Orville laid it out for him, though, Harvey was mildly relieved. Compared to what he'd been expecting, the task assigned to him seemed tolerable, if not rewarding, in its own perverse way.

He had his chance to carry out his mission between first and second periods at school that morning, when he managed to track down Dickie in the throng of students crowding the hallway.

"Hey, Dickie!" he cried out, elbowing his way to his archenemy's side. "How's it going?" he asked pleasantly.

"It's going north by northeast, to chemistry class," Dickie said stiffly. "What do you want, Harvey?"

"Well, uh, I . . ."

"Spit it out, Peterjohn," Dickie demanded. "I'm a busy kid."

"Yeah, right." Harvey laughed uncomfortably, tugging at his collar. "Dickie, it's such a hot day, I thought maybe you'd like to come up to my mansion for a swim. You can bring your lovely sisters with you. . . ."

"*Your* mansion?" Dickie retorted.

"You know what I mean," Harvey said, still trying to smile through his discomfort. "It's just sort of a peace gesture, you know? To make up for me getting you booted out of school."

"Hey, you think I was complaining about being suspended?" Dickie said, heading for his next class as Harvey stayed doggedly at his side.

"Whatever. Do you want to come by?"

"Well, we've got a pretty full schedule," Dickie said. "But maybe we can stop in for a minute. . . ."

"That'd be great!" Harvey said, trying to muster some genuine enthusiasm.

"Harvey," Dickie asked him. "Are you feeling okay? This isn't like you, you know."

"Just trying to be a nice guy," Harvey said, breaking away from Dickie. "See ya after school, then, right?"

"Yeah, probably."

Before going in to his class, Dickie watched Harvey vanish into the thick of the other students. Bette emerged into view from the roving mass and hurried to her brother's side.

"What were you talking to Harvey Peterjohn about?" she asked him.

"He wants us to come swimming at his old man's pool after school today," Dickie said.

"Come on, you can't be serious!" Bette said. "What happened, did he buy some piranha he wants to test on us?"

"Yeah, I'm a little suspicious myself," Dickie admitted. "I say we check it out, but we ought to be on our toes. It could be a trap. You know what they say: Like son, like father."

"I think it's the other way around, Dickie."

Twenty

If the Olympics were ever to be held in Ramona, the swimming events would most likely be staged in Orville Peterjohn's backyard, where there was a pool large enough to float a small armada and still have room left over for a handful of challengers to wage the battle of the breaststroke. Today, though, the level of activity was minimal. The Cessna children were enjoying the pool and its surroundings under the basking warmth of the midday sun. June had the pool to herself and floated luxuriously about on an inflated raft, trying to supplement her farmer's tan with a little color on those parts of her body that were usually covered during workshifts in the manure pile. Bette and NeNe were in the nearby Jacuzzi, splashing each other when they weren't tickling themselves with jets of hot water surging from underwater ducts. On the large expanse of bluegrass lawn around the pool, Dickie was amusing himself with a croquet mallet, chasing wooden balls through hoops in the ground.

Orville watched the kids from the patio, where he was standing guard over a half dozen hamburgers sizzling above the flames in a mammoth brick fireplace.

"Why don't you go play with them, Harvey," he goaded his son. "Make them feel comfortable."

"They look plenty comfortable to me," Harvey said, standing next to his father. "I'll just wait until these burgers are ready to serve."

"Well, wait no longer." Orville was in far better spirits than he had been earlier that morning. He was sure that handling the Cessna kids would be one of his easier conquests. They already looked buttered up enough for him to move ahead with his plan. He gestured for his son to grab a platter loaded with opened buns, then began prying hamburgers from the grill as he called out, "Snacks are being served on the patio! Come and get it!"

By the time all the burgers had been nestled into their respective buns, the youthful Kidco executives were all gathered around an umbrella-shaded table a few yards from the grill. As Harvey swallowed his pride and played the part of waiter, carrying the platter so that the others could choose their burgers, Orville sat down next to Dickie and snapped his fingers for the family servant to dispense soft drinks to the guests.

There was a moment's silence as everyone began to eat, then the Peterjohn's bulldog announced its arrival from the side yard, growling lowly as it lugged its burly frame across the patio tiles toward the table. When NeNe leaned back and reached out to pet the dog, Brutus stopped short and spread its mouth to reveal sharp yellow teeth. NeNe jerked her hand back to her side, but not before Brutus barked loudly and snapped his jaws in the vicinity of her fingers.

"Brutus!" Orville scolded. "Bad dog!"

"He almost bit me!" NeNe exclaimed.

"He probably smelled the hamburgers and thought you were offering him one," Harvey said offhandedly, fighting back his urge to commend Brutus on a job well done.

"I don't know what's gotten into him today," Orville apologized. "Normally, he *loves* children."

Harvey coughed, then buried his face in his hamburger.

Dickie stole a sidelong glance at Orville between bites, trying to calculate the man's strategy. So far, he'd been amiable to the point of excess, and Dickie knew that for anybody like Orville Peterjohn to put on that long and that good a show took considerable effort. There had to be a reason for it, and Dickie was wary of waiting for that reason to emerge on its own.

"This is really swell of you, Mr. Peterjohn," he prompted. "You sure seem to be going out of your way to show us a good time . . . and succeeding, too, of course!"

"It's my pleasure," Orville said grandly. "As a fellow businessman, I wanted to celebrate Kidco's success—"

"Excuse me," Bette interrupted, pointing out her sisters to Orville. "We're business*persons*."

"I stand corrected," Orville said, smiling with mock embarrassment. "As a fellow business*person*," he resumed, now addressing all four of the Cessna children, "I also have to *do* something about that success. You see, you're taking away my customers. . . ."

Dickie stopped chewing in midbite and looked across the table at his sisters. NeNe lowered her burger to her plate, and both June and Bette returned Dickie's glance with glances of their own. From the expressions on their faces, one might have thought the Cessnas had either just come down with food poisoning or found out that their burgers were made from one of their old mares that had died the previous winter.

"Relax," Orville told them, still smiling graciously as he clasped his hands together before him, adopting what he liked to refer to as his wheel-and-deal pose. "I have a proposition that I think will make us all happy. Quite simply, I want to buy all the fertilizer you produce, every month, at the same price you're charging now. You won't lose a penny, and I can get back my old accounts. That's fair enough, isn't it?"

Dickie had been anticipating a number of tricks Orville might have had up his sleeves, but this wasn't one of them. Caught off guard by the proposal, he could only stare at the man who had delivered it. Orville was grinning like a chessmaster who'd just whispered "Checkmate."

"Mr. Peterjohn," Dickie said hoarsely, once he found his voice. "Does that mean we'd be working for *you*?"

Orville scanned the faces of the four children watching him, easily spotting their foremost objection. "No, it doesn't have to be me," he offered, glancing over at his son. "I could put Harvey in charge of it."

"Harvey?" Dickie said, screwing up his face as if he'd just bit into a lemon. His sisters reacted with equal discomfort, although they kept silent. Harvey squirmed restlessly in his chair. At a lower altitude, Brutus shuffled a few steps sideways and growled at its master's son.

"Well, we can work out something, I'm sure," Orville bargained once more.

Without bothering to consult his sisters, Dickie set down his burger and wove his own hands together, mimicking Orville's posture as he said, "Sorry, Mr. Peterjohn, but we work alone. We don't need any grown-ups coming in and taking over."

June stretched her leg out under the table and gave Dickie a sharp kick to get his attention, then shook her head vigorously to protest. It was too late, though. Orville had reached the limit of what passed with him for the milk of human kindness. The edges of his mouth drooped into a scowl, and his eyebrows arched like shifting weights, pressing his eyelids down until he was staring at the children through thin, glinting pupils.

"You better understand something, all of you," he said, forsaking all pretense at conviviality. "To me you're not just a bunch of enterprising kids. To me, you're competition."

Intimidated by the sudden change in Orville's demeanor, June and Bette cowered back in their seats. NeNe gulped, looking at her brother for assistance. Dickie's confidence wavered for a moment, but he bolstered it with a shot of courage and faced up to Orville's implied challenge.

"Well, may the best corporation win," Dickie said, rising to his feet. "We better get going now. We have a lot of work to do. Come on, girls. . . ."

Eager to escape the tension of the confrontation, June, Bette and NeNe leaped from their seats and joined Dickie in a mass exodus from the patio.

"Thanks for everything, Mr. Peterjohn," Bette said with forced politeness. "See you in school, Harvey."

As the Cessnas hopped onto their bikes and rode off in unison, Orville sighed loudly with irritation. Beside him,

Harvey hoisted his hamburger and prepared to bite into it, first telling his father, "I bet they don't even write us thank-you notes."

Orville lashed out with the back of his hand, sending the burger flying from Harvey's hand as he shouted with frustration, "Those weren't for you!"

Brutus was quick to pounce on the fallen patty, wolfing it down voraciously. The servant drifted over, sidestepping the bulldog as he began to remove the unfinished soft drinks from the table. Pouting sullenly, Harvey reached behind him with a fork and discreetly prodded Brutus's hindquarters. Letting out a yip of outrage, the dog whirled around and fixed its angry eyes on the servant.

"Now, Brutus, it wasn't I who . . ." The servant let the rest of the sentence dangle, choosing instead to retreat from the bulldog's jaw-snapping assault. Like refugees from a silent movie, they engaged in pathetic chase across the patio to the pool, where the servant took the only possible avenue of escape and plunged headlong into the water.

"I suppose you didn't think I saw you do that," Orville told his son.

"Sorry, Dad," Harvey said, looking down at his plate.

"I bet you are," Orville grumbled.

Twenty-one

The heat wave was still sitting on Ramona the following Saturday morning. There was a lulling swelter in the air, the kind of beating heat that makes the body long to take it easy. From the looks of the Cessna children, they were following just such an urge. NeNe was playing jacks on the front porch, punctuating the lazy quiet with the steady thunk of a small rubber ball. Behind her, June and Frank were swinging on the porch swing, arms around one another, watching the day go by. Bette lay in a hammock strung across the uprights at the other end of the porch, absorbed in a Nancy Drew mystery about a missing pendant.

The serenity was shattered soon after by the arrival of Dickie, who strolled purposefully out the front door, dressed for work and clapping his hands like an animal trainer signaling for his brood of tigers to rear on their hind legs.

"Okay, everybody! Time to get cracking!" he rooted vigorously. When he noticed that his enthusiasm wasn't being matched by the others, he paused, looking his sisters over. "Come on, come on. Another day, another dollar. June, you and Bette take the stables. Me and NeNe will get the golf cart. . . ."

NeNe looked up at her brother, jiggling jacks in the palm of her hand. Bette peered at him over the top of her book. June yawned. None of them said a word or made any move to get up from where they were.

"Don't strain yourselves on my account," Dickie told them caustically, putting his hands on his hips.

"Dickie, aren't you getting a little bossy?" June said, unanchoring Frank's arm from her shoulder.

"And a little stupid," Bette joined in the assault. "Showing off like that in front of Mr. Peterjohn?"

"Hey, that was one president to another," Dickie defended himself. "And let me tell you something about Peterjohn... you can bet *he's* not laying around on his ass today!"

"Who cares?" NeNe sulked, spreading out her jacks and then bouncing the ball while she grabbed back as many as she could before it landed.

"You should, that's who," Dickie said. "We've got a challenge before us. Kidco's got a reputation to live up to now!"

"You mean Dickie Cessna's got a reputation to live up to!" Bette retorted.

"Hey, come on . . . what's going on here?" Dickie pointed to Bette. "Neil's article on Kidco's going to be in the paper first thing next week. How do you think it's going to look if word gets out that the whole thing's a big sham and that we're not really all that committed to doing a top-notch job, huh?"

Dickie had said the magic words. Bette set down her book and swung her legs out of the hammock. "Okay," she conceded, "I'll get to work. I just think we all should have had a say before you turned down Mr. Peterjohn's offer. I mean, if he bought all the fertilizer we could make, we wouldn't have to do any advertising or spend more of our profits on expand—"

"It woulda been a sellout!" Dickie said. "Don't you see? Old man Peterjohn wants the whole fertilizer business to himself, so he can charge what he wants and give people a hard time and run a big monopoly and all that other stuff! We're making a stand for free enterprise and the American Way!"

"You forgot Mom and apple pie," June said, reluctantly getting up from the porch swing and sighing. "All right, Dickie. You win. Let's go make ourselves miserable."

"Wonderful," Frank drawled bitterly, rising to his feet. "Doesn't anyone ever get a day off around here?"

"You do," Dickie told him. "Unless, of course, you might be interested in being subcontracted to help us out."

"No, no, that's okay," Frank said, shaking his head as he headed down the steps. "Horseshit just isn't my forte."

"No, but bullsh—"

"Look!" Bette shrieked suddenly, cutting short Dickie's insult. She was pointing at the front flower beds, and the others looked to see a gopher venturing unsteadily from its hole.

"Oh no!" NeNe gasped.

The gopher straggled away from the flower bed and onto the lawn, its motions becoming increasingly awkward. Finally, it struggled up onto its hind legs, took a few perfunctory whiffs of the morning air, then keeled over onto the grass.

"Goofer!" NeNe cried out, sending her jacks flying as she rushed past Frank to the fallen rodent's side.

"Goofer?" Dickie mumbled to himself as he came over to take a look. As NeNe looked on in abject misery, Dickie picked up a stick and gently prodded the gopher.

"Is . . . is he . . . ?" NeNe whispered despondently.

"He's cashed in," Dickie announced, tossing the stick aside. "How weird . . ."

"I killed him!" NeNe wailed, lunging to her feet. "I killed Goofer!" Approaching hysteria, she reached for her hair, and June had to rush to her side to keep her from trying to pull it out. "I'm a murderer!" NeNe wept. "Put me in the 'lectric chair! Bury me alive!"

"Hey, take it easy, NeNe," June told her.

As Dickie continued to stare at the gopher, Bette joined

him, curiosity overcoming her revulsion. Neither of them said anything for a few seconds, then they looked at each another simultaneously.

"Are you thinking what I'm thinking?" Bette asked Dickie.

"Probably." They went over to their grief-stricken sister, and Dickie asked her, "NeNe! How did you kill that gopher?"

"Get me a blindfold!" NeNe whimpered. "Bring on the firing squad!"

"NeNe!" Bette said, shaking her sister. When that didn't snap NeNe out of her hysterics, Bette relied on her television training and slapped her in the face, shouting, "Tell us how!"

NeNe ceased her weeping instantly and stared at Bette incredulously, then shot her own hand out and returned the slap as she sniffled, "I'll show you. . . ."

As Frank abandoned the scene and headed for his car, the Cessna children filed into the house, following NeNe to the kitchen, where she opened the cupboard where the brown sugar was kept.

"I was feeding this to Goofer for the past few weeks," she explained. "We got to be buddies, sort of like secret—"

"Then *you're* the one who's been springing the traps," Dickie said, taking the box of sugar from NeNe. "Boy, would Dad tan your fanny if he found out!"

"You won't tell him, will you?" NeNe pleaded.

"Not if you tell us everything about this," Dickie said, shaking the box. "If you were feeding him this stuff for weeks, how come he suddenly up and died today?"

"I don't know!" NeNe said. "Last night, I was helping Mom unclog the sink, and then when she had to go next door for a plunger, I snuck out and fed Goofer. Only this time when I gave him the sugar, he made a little cough. I knew something was wrong!"

"But that doesn't make any sense," Dickie said. "Brown sugar's not fatal. . . ."

"Maybe Goofer was a diabetic," NeNe theorized, bringing herself under control.

When they were interrupted by a banging on the kitchen door, the children looked over and saw Frank standing outside, staring through the window.

"June!" he called out. "Will ya let me in? I decided to hang around. . . ."

June looked at her brother, who shook his head decisively.

"This is official Kidco business," he insisted, becoming swept up by a newfound burst of enthusiasm. "Ramona's one big gopher hole, from the country club to our own front yard. If NeNe's found some way to take care of gophers, it'll make us as much money as manure!"

"Juney!" Frank shouted above his renewed knocking. "Open up!"

"I . . . I can't, Frank," she told him. "This is Kidco business, like Dickie said."

"The hell with Kidco!" Frank pounded his fist one last time on the door, then stomped off angrily.

"Frank!" June called out, heading for the door.

"Take it easy, June," Dickie called out to her. "You'll have plenty of time to visit that deadbeat when I put him in debtor's prison."

June watched from the doorway as Frank drove off, but decided against going after him. She rejoined the conclave gathered around the sink, where Dickie was inspecting the box of brown sugar.

Wiping tears from her eyes, NeNe said, "They told us at school that too much sugar's bad for you. It must be true for—"

"NeNe!" Dickie interrupted, sorting through a palmful of sugar and coming upon a few albino crystals of a different consistency. "You said you were helping Mom unclog the sink?"

"Yeah . . ."

Dickie isolated the white chunks and held them up for the others to see as he told NeNe, "You're lucky you didn't poison everybody!"

Upending the box, Dickie dumped the rest of the brown sugar in the sink, revealing more white crystals, then knelt down and opened the cabinet doors below.

"What is it, Dickie?" Bette asked.

Finding what he was looking for, Dickie pulled out a cylindrical can and held it aloft next to the emptied box, announcing, "The greatest discovery since Frosted Flakes—brown sugar . . . and Dranol"

"Huh?" June said.

"You heard me," Dickie said. "Look, here's our big chance to branch out our operations! What an opportunity! You know that famous saying? 'Build a better mousetrap and the world will beat a path to your door'? Well, the same goes for gophers! Mark my words!"

"First horse manure, now dead gophers," June said whimsically. "How glamorous can you get. . . ."

Twenty-two

A newly made sign declared to the world in general that the San Diego Country Estates Equestrian Stables also housed Kidco Corporate Headquarters. The lettering had been done with a stencil, nice and neat, except for the fact that the spacing between letters had been miscalculated so that the tail end of Headquarters was jammed together like a pressed accordion.

Inside a partitioned-off section of the feed room, the children had set up the company laboratory. In the full spirit of their new enterprise, Dickie was wearing a full-length white smock, looking every bit the small-scale scientist. Working as his research assistant, NeNe had on a T-shirt with the imprint of a laboratory jacket stamped on its front.

"Sugar . . ." Dickie called out, extending one hand

"Poor Goofer," NeNe reflected.

"'Poor Goofer'?" Dickie said. "NeNe, he wound up with a product named after him. Even Bambi never got that!"

"I guess you're right."

"Of course I'm right," Dickie said, taking a sheet of paper and rolling it into a funnel. Fitting the narrow end inside the mouth of the Drano can, he emptied out the contents of the beaker, then capped the can and handed it back to Bette so she could glue the new label into place.

Just then June poked her head up through the opening where the ladder reached the loft. "Hey, are you guys ready?" she asked. "Frank's ready to take us to see Mr. Clark."

"Coming!" Dickie said, staring fondly at their new product. On impulse, he kissed the label, then told the girls, "All right! Let's go make ourselves our second fortune!"

As usual, Frank was in no mood for the constant banter of shoptalk that the Cessna children began trading as they rode to the other side of the Estates. "Bad enough I have to get suckered into being your chauffeur," he complained, glaring at Dickie in the rearview mirror. "Do I have to put up with all this squawking, too? Kidco this, Kidco that... you're all getting to be a royal pain in the butt."

"Oh, is that a fact?" June said haughtily, edging away from Frank in the front seat.

"I'm not talking about you, June," Frank said quickly, pulling into the main parking lot for the golf course. "It's just that I think I should be able to date you without feeling like I'm barging in on a business meeting all the time. I mean, there are other things in life besides making a buck."

"Or ten bucks, plus interest," Dickie cracked.

"Shut up, Dickie!" Frank said as he pulled to a stop near the guest lodge. "You precocious little snot!"

"Frank!" June gasped.

"What's precocious mean?" NeNe asked.

"It means somebody with a swollen head asking for a fat lip," Frank snarled, staying in the car while the others piled out. He pointed a warning finger at Dickie and said. "You'll get yours, just wait!"

"I don't like threats," Dickie said.

"Yeah, well, I don't like being made fun of all the time just because I feel like enjoying my youth," Frank said. "You guys want to be in a big rush to grow up, be my guest! But count me out!"

As Frank screeched off, Dickie made a face at the retreating car and sneered. "That guy sure is jealous."

"Leave him alone," June said. "He's right about you, Dickie. You *do* get more obnoxious than you have to be sometimes."

"Well, I'm in business to make money, not friends," Dickie affirmed as they headed up the steps to Clark's office. "I can't help the way I am...."

"You could *try* to be nicer to Frank," June told him. "He *is* my boyfriend, after all."

"Okay, okay," Dickie said. "I won't charge him any interest on the money he owes me. How's that for being a nice guy?"

"My heart is melting."

"Now that that's settled, let's get down to business," Dickie said.

They had called for an appointment with Mr. Clark, and he welcomed them warmly into his office. Dickie showed him their new product and delivered a sales pitch to go along with the abbreviated contract Kidco had drawn up to cover their gopher-killing services. Clark nodded his head approvingly once the whole presentation had been made, then picked up the phone and dialed a number from his Rolodex.

"Hello, Morton?" he said into the receiver as he grinned over at the kids. "Clark here. I just wanted to tell you that you can cross us off your list of clients, as of today. . . . That's right, Morton, you're being replaced. . . . Why do you think? There're so many goddamn holes on my golf course I'm beginning to think you're a double agent for the gophers! Now, good luck elsewhere, but you're through here! Goodbye!"

Dickie looked over at his sisters, beaming. They all seemed equally elated, including June, who offered her brother a grudging smile.

"Okay, you're on," Clark told them after he hung up the phone and graced the contract with his signature. "At two dollars a gopher hole, you'll probably make enough money to retire from the front nine alone."

"I don't think we're ready to retire yet, Mr. Clark," Dickie said, taking back his copy of the contract along with their can of Kidco Goofer Gopher Killer.

"Yeah," Bette said. "Add us all together and we're only forty-eight!"

"Interesting observation," Clark said, getting up from his chair and going over to the window. Pointing at the golf course, he said, "Well, no reason why you can't start right in, is there?"

"No, sir!" Dickie said. "Come on, ladies, let's go show those gophers we mean business!"

They started on the first green. Since it was groundskeeping day, the course was closed to golfers, and they only had to work around the men mowing the fairways and mending sprinkler lines. Spreading out, they slowly advanced down the fairway, keeping their eyes open for telltale signs of gopher infiltration. In each instance when they came upon a hole, they would use a trowel to widen the opening slightly, then pour in a bit of their secret concoction before pounding dirt over the hole. It took them nearly an hour to reach the green. While Bette and June tended to the openings at the edge of the nearest sand trap, Dickie poisoned a hole on the green itself. When he finished, he looked over and saw NeNe poised over the pin, staring into the first hole cup.

"NeNe," Dickie said as he paced over. "Any hole that's got a flag in it is *supposed* to be there."

"Oh yeah?" NeNe said, pointing to the cup, where a minute showering of dirt flew out of the opening as a gopher burrowed its way to sunlight. Dickie stared with wonder at the small, furry creature, then hurried over to the hole. The gopher popped back inside its borrowed lair.

"We got a door prize for you, gopher," Dickie said, shaking some of the mixture into the hole. "It's nothing personal, you understand. With any luck, maybe you'll be reincarnated as a horse and we can end up being partners. . . ."

Twenty-three

It was fortunate for the children that the school year ended concurrently with the development of their new product and service, because once word got around about the efficiency of Kidco Goofer Gopher Killer, the young Cessnas found themselves beseiged by offers to work their wonders elsewhere in town. If not the whole world, it seemed at least as if all Ramona was beating a path to their door. Most noteworthy of their new clients was none other than Principal Ruggles, who stoically paid out his two dollars to Dickie and NeNe for eliminating the one pest that had given him more aggravation than they had at school. In the face of this influx of new business, the children were forced to forsake their exclusive partnership and begin hiring friends on a part-time basis to help them keep up with the demand for their services. Even Frank quit criticizing and agreed to put in a few hours to pay off his debt to Dickie and make enough to take June out on a few dates without her having to foot the bill.

The fertilizer business continued to prosper as well, particularly on alternate weekends, when the steady stream of trucks making their way down Oaktree Lane would guarantee that by the end of the day the mountain of existing manure would be reduced to a molehill. The cashbox filled up so quickly during the ensuing weeks that the kids decided to invest in a large safe, which they placed in the corner of their "laboratory" and regularly fed with the latest grosses. Then, inevitably, came the day when the safe itself became filled to the point of bursting, requiring another solution. The children didn't have to put their heads together for long to decide what to do....

To celebrate the milestone of Harvey Peterjohn's thirteenth birthday, Orville took his son to his favorite place of worship, the Ramona branch of the Bank of America. Arriving at the decorous institution, the Peterjohns were ushered past the throng of other customers waiting in long lines for their chance to handle transactions with the two tellers on duty. George Theo Sones, the branch manager, was waiting for them in his office. He was a bureaucratic-looking man of indeterminable age, wearing a freshly pressed suit and a look of practiced benevolence.

"Mr. Peterjohn, Harvey," he said passing his hand around. "So good of you to come. I have the forms all prepared for you. I realize how valuable your time is."

"Fine, George, fine," Orville boomed merrily, taking a seat next to the manager's desk and motioning for his son to do the same. As he skimmed over the form George handed him and filled in the appropriate information, he said, "I figure a young man entering his teens is about ready for his own bank account. We'll start it off with twenty-five dollars."

"This must be a big day for you, Harvey," George said to the boy, who was shifting restlessly in his chair.

"Yes, sir," Harvey said, sounding like a talking doll whose string had just been pulled. "A penny saved is a penny earned."

"A very wise saying," George said, taking the papers from Orville and double-checking all the entries, at the same time asking the older man, "Speaking of saving, I've noticed your deposits have been getting increasingly smaller lately, Orville. Business on the downswing?"

Orville's mood immediately darkened and he barked, "I didn't come here to discuss *my* financial affairs, George."

"Of course," George said, smiling flimsily. "I shouldn't have pried. Forgive me."

"If you must know, we're reinvesting, making some big expansion plans," Orville claimed.

"But, Dad, I thought that things were going bad on account—"

"Enough, Harvey!" Orville cut in, clamping his hand over his son's mouth. "No one solicited your opinion."

As Orville was pulling his hand away, the door to George's office creaked open and a subordinate officer poked his head in, saying, "Mr. Sones, excuse me, but there's a—"

"Jenkins, can't you see I'm busy with Mr. Peterjohn and little Mr. Peterjohn?" George snapped with irritation.

Letting himself in, Jenkins flushed red as he slithered across the carpet to his superior's side, lowering his voice. "I see, but I thought you'd want to know about this new account. . . ."

George looked out the door and the Peterjohns leaned forward in their seats to see where Jenkins was pointing. Just outside the office, the Cessna children stood flanking the Kidco wagon, which was heaped high with bulging bags adorned with dollar signs. Skip Russo was with them, wearing a trenchcoat a few sizes too large for him. He had the collar turned up and one hand tucked inside the coat, like Napoleon.

"They want to deposit. . . thirty thousand dollars!" Jenkins whispered, incredulous.

"Why, those damn little shots!" Orville fumed, scowling at his competitors.

"And my account's for a measly twenty-five bucks," Harvey muttered downheartedly.

Adjusting his tie, George got up from his seat and flashed the Peterjohns an apologetic smile, saying, "You'll have to excuse me a moment." Moving away from his desk and heading for the money, he snapped his fingers, ordering, "Jenkins! Get some security over here!"

Throwing open his coat, Skip withdrew his hand, which was clenched tightly around the handle of a baseball bat. He swung it in such a way as to suggest that he was capable of using it to hit more than home runs.

"Security's taken care of," he told the branch manager.

"This is too much!" Orville roared with contempt. The closest thing he could take out his frustration on was the form he'd just filled out on behalf of his son, and he ripped it savagely in half.

"Dad!" Harvey cried out. "That's my acc—"

"Come on!" Orville said, lunging to his feet and taking Harvey by the hand, jerking the youth from his seat. They stormed out of the office under the full force of Orville's wrath, and he bored his livid gaze into the eyes of the Cessna children as he barreled past them. Harvey straggled behind, awkwardly struggling to keep his balance. He looked like something tied to the rear end of a newlywed's car the day of their wedding.

"There goes one sore loser," Dickie observed with a trace of a smile.

"Won't you all step into my office?" George bade them, gesturing inside. "So good of you to come. . . ."

Twenty-four

By the time school resumed in the fall, the Cessna children were almost grateful for the change of pace. The summer had been anything but a vacation, and compared to the relentless pursuit of gophers and the interminable shoveling of never-ending heaps of horse manure, sitting at a desk and listening to a teacher lecture had a wistful allure to it. Of the four kids, Bette's return to classes was accompanied by the most anticipation. After all, she'd gotten a call the day before from Neil Brody, who'd requested an interview with her during lunch period, since he was looking for a story to feature in the first issue of the *Ramona Day Bugle* and decided that the way the Cessnas had spent their summer vacation was the best copy around.

Rather than douse herself with perfume and don an Easter outfit, this time Bette was determined to try another approach and play hard-to-get. She wore her regular school outfit, and carried herself through her morning classes with an aura of self-confidence and assurance. The fact that almost every other student she came in contact with had something to say about Kidco didn't hurt matters any. By lunchtime, she was ready to stride into the cafeteria and be so aloof with Neil Brody that he wouldn't be able to help but fall madly in love with her.

Of course, reality being the great equalizer that it is, the moment Bette *did* walk through the door into the lunchroom, she was beset by an almost paralyzing fear. Spotting Neil at the same table where they'd talked the previous spring, Bette felt her cool facade falling away from her like snakeskin in molting season. By the time she sat down across from him to begin the interview, she was playing about as hard-to-get as hickies in Transylvania.

Neil was much the same as he'd been during the last interview, the model of uninvolved efficiency, rattling off all the right questions and condensing Bette's nervous, rambling remarks into all the right answers. Thirteen years old and already he was a seasoned veteran.

"So, it was a real prosperous summer for Kidco," Bette said in conclusion, watching, inwardly begging Neil to look up from his pad and pay some attention to her.

"Um hmmmmm," he mumbled incoherently as he raced his pencil across his notebook, getting down the last batch of facts Bette had given him.

"As a matter of fact, we're thinking of getting into communications," Bette said, trying to stretch out the interview. "So, if someone wanted to ask me out for a date, and he happened to be a newspaperman, I could write it off as a business expense. . . ."

"Um hmmmmm," Neil murmured, getting it all down . . . on paper, at least. Bette could have taken lessons from him about how to play hard-to-get.

"He wouldn't have to pay a *penny,*" Bette said, urgency weighing heavily in her voice.

"Okay, thanks," Neil said perfunctorily, closing his notebook and rising to his feet. "Nice talking to you again, Bette."

"Oh, so you know my name," Bette said, resorting to sarcasm in her desperation.

"Of course," Neil said. "What a silly thing to say. . . ."

Bette remained seated, watching Neil walk off. The feeling of *déjà vu* was overpowering. Unlike last time, however, she refused to cry. Sucking in a deep breath, she forced down the surge of emotion that had been welling up inside her.

"Well, well, if it isn't ol' Bette Cessna!"

Bette whirled around in her seat and saw Harvey Peterjohn strolling toward her, a cocky swagger to his gait and a grin on his face.

"Hello, Harvey," Bette said dully, looking away from him in hope that he'd keep on walking past the table.

No such luck. He stopped next to Bette and stared down at her, his arms folded across his chest. "Everywhere I go around school, all I hear is people talking about how neat Kidco is and how they all want to form their own little corporations. You must feel good about that, huh?"

"Why do you ask, Harvey?" Bette asked innocently.

Harvey answered her question with another question. "Have you or the rest of your family ever wondered why my dad hasn't done anything to try to stop you from cutting into his business all this time?"

"It's probably because there's nothing he *can* do," Bette said. "It's a free country. He can't stop us."

"Oh, I don't know about that," Harvey said, his grin widening.

"What are you getting at?" Bette demanded.

"Nothing," Harvey laughed lightly. "It's nothing."

Bette was going to press further, but Dickie came into the cafeteria and quickly made his way over to the table, matching Harvey's smirk with one of his own.

"How's it goin', Harve?" Dickie said. "You over here to invite us over to your pool again or something?"

"Are you kidding?" Harvey sniffed. "The water's still polluted from last time you were by."

"Hey, that's pretty funny... for you, that is," Dickie said. "What happened, did you take advanced insults at summer school along with all the classes you flunked?"

Harvey was stymied. While he tried to untie his tongue and come up with a suitable retort, Bette looked over at her brother and said, "Harvey was telling me his father's going to try to get even with us somehow for taking away business from him."

"Oh yeah?" Dickie said. He leveled a threatening gaze at Harvey and warned, "Well, we got enough money to fight back against anything you or your Pa want to throw at us, and don't you forget it!"

"That's not all I won't forget," Harvey promised, then strode out of the cafeteria.

"What do you think?" Bette asked Dickie once they were alone. "Do you think we should be worried about Mr. Peterjohn?"

"I think mostly Harvey's full of hot air," Dickie guessed. "I bet his dad wishes there was something he could do, but since there isn't, that's as far as it will go."

"I hope you're right," Bette said.

"Aren't I always?" Dickie boasted.

"Let your head swell any more, Dickie, and you won't be able to wear any of your hats," Bette said. Getting to her feet, she said, "I just hope Harvey was only bluffing."

Twenty-five

It was only a matter of time before word about the exploits of Kidco cleared the Cuyamacas and spread across the land. In particular, the word found its way into the Los Angeles production offices for the Sunday morning television show *Kids Are the Darnedest People*. The show's producer was nibbling his way through a take-out order of sushi as he studied a clipboard containing the tentative lineup for the next weekend's show. Across the desk from him, his assistant leafed through a master file containing potential story items. Outside the window, warm winds stirred the fronds of a towering palm tree.

"Okay," the producer said, swallowing a mouthful of squid. "We got the spelling bee champ, the kid from that new comedy series, and the thirteen-year-old going to UCLA. We still need one more. . . ."

"Try this on for size," his assistant said, taking a clipping from the file. "From the *Ramona Day Bugle* . . . some school paper, from the looks of it. There's this brother and three sisters who run a corporation called Kidco. They sell horse manure and kill gophers. . . ."

"I dunno," the producer said. "Horse manure . . . it's unappetizing." Fingering his chopsticks, he probed one of the take-out containers for the last of the fisheyes.

"Well, get a load of this," his assistant said, reading from the article, "'Executive Secretary Bette Cessna confided to the *Bugle* that Kidco this summer cleared more than six thousand dollars a month!'"

"Say what?" the producer gasped, losing his grip on the fisheye as he reached out with his free hand for the news clipping. . . .

The following weekend, the Cessna children were on the set, wearing their Sunday best as they waited for a commercial break to end. June looked terrified, Bette merely bashful. NeNe was squinting past the floodlights for a glimpse at the youthful audience gathered for the taping. Dickie stared down at his opened palm, where he'd written out a series of memorable quotes that he hoped would ensure him a shot at instant immortality. The show's host, Stu Stone, looked as if he'd just wandered across the lot from playing a stunt double on *Hawaii Five-O*. He was all tan, blow-dried hair and print shirt, with capped teeth and the sincerity of a politician on election eve.

When the show's director cued Stu that the cameras would be rolling in ten seconds, he looked over at the kids and whispered, "Okay, gang, knock 'em dead!"

June looked over at her brother in a way that suggested she wanted nothing better than to press some hidden button that would eject her from the proceedings. Dickie waved for her to stay calm, then tightened his tie and straightened the lapels of his corduroy sport coat as he sat upright in his seat and stared intently at the three cameras taking in the activity on the set. When the red monitor light flashed on above one of the cameras, Stu grinned at it, lapsing into his automated enthusiasm.

"All right, kids! We have for you now four of the darnedest guests we've ever had!" he gushed, playing up to the stage audience. "Would you like to meet them right now?"

"YEAHHHHHH!" a few dozen children howled in unison from their seats, responding to the arm-waving cues of both Stu and the show's producer, who stood just out of camera range.

Swaggering over to his guests, Stu clasped his hands together, saying, "Hi! Why don't you tell everybody here, and all the viewers at home, just who you are!?"

"We are Kidco," Dickie said, beaming into the camera.

Among the thousands of television sets tuned into *Kids Are the Darnedest People* throughout the state was the wide-screened Advent taking up half the wall in Orville Peterjohn's living room. Besides his son, Orville had invited a guest to watch the program, Phil Porzinski of the State Board of Taxation. While the two men sat in plush chairs, staring contemptuously at the screen, Harvey was stretched out on the floor, obviously displeased with the fare on the tube.

"Daaaaad," he whined, looking back at Orville. "Can't we watch something else . . . ?"

"Shut up, Harvey, or I'll lock you in the basement," Orville warned.

On the screen, the Cessna children introduced themselves individually, stating their positions within the firm of Kidco. When they were finished, the cameras panned back to Stu, who turned once more to exhort the youthful throng in the studio audience.

"To give you an idea of how Kidco works, we sent our crew to their hometown. Would you like to see what they brought back?"

"YEAAAAHHHHHH!" came the rehearsed cheer.

The screen blacked out for a fraction of a second, then filled with the image of the Cessna's tract home as Stu provided the offscreen narration.

"Dickie, NeNe, Bette, and June live in this house in Ramona, California, a small town forty miles northeast of San Diego. . . ."

"Son-of-a-bitch!" Porzinski muttered angrily, blowing smoke from his cigarette as he glared at the screen. "I *knew* those little shits were running a scam on us!"

Orville glanced over at Porzinski, puffing complacently on his cigar now, pleased with the tax man's reaction.

As the image on the screen shifted to the stables and surrounding equestrian center, Stu narrated, "Their dad, Richard Cessna Senior, works at the San Diego Country

Estates, where he takes care of one hundred and seventy horses used for trail rides, horse shows and thoroughbred racing. . . ."

Brutus, who had been dozing up to now at Orville's feet, suddenly perked up his prunish face and growled unpleasantly at the television, where Bette and June were now being shown shoveling manure and straw under the rays of the afternoon sun.

"Easy, Brutus," Orville said, reaching down to pet the bulldog. "Shhhhhh."

Stu wrapped up his voice-over narrative. "One hundred and seventy horses make a huge amount of . . . well, you know what! Kidco mixes it with straw, lets it compost, then sells it to farmers and landscapers as fertilizer! And that's just one of Kidco's enterprises . . . !"

Orville grabbed the remote control switchbox from the armrest and turned down the sound, then looked over at Porzinski, taking his cigar out of his mouth as he spoke. "When my research into the Cessnas uncovered your . . . involvement with them, I realized you'd probably want to watch this program."

Porzinski nodded, letting twin streams of smoke spill from his nose. "I appreciate your calling me, Mr. Peterjohn. . . ."

"Please. Orville," the older man said indulgently, reaching to the table between them and pouring Porzinski another drink from a pitcherful of chilled martinis.

They turned their attention back to the screen and Orville turned up the volume. The film clip segment was over, and now the Cessna children were fielding questions from the audience, where Stu was poking his microphone into the face of a girl NeNe's age. She asked, "What are you gonna do with all your money?"

"Well, we're thinking of a college," Dickie answered quickly.

"You hear that, everyone?" Stu enthused, mugging for the camera. "They're using their money to buy the most valuable gift in the world, a college education!"

As the audience cheered, Dickie shook his head, speaking above the applause, "No, what we want to do is *buy* a college! We don't think they're teaching the right stuff, so we want to take over!"

Properly incited, the children spectators roared their

approval, throwing in a few wolf-whistles and catcalls. Dickie basked in the ovation, paying no attention to the jealous glances cast his way by his three sisters.

"I think we've seen enough, don't you think, Phil?" Orville said. When Porzinski nodded, Orville snapped off the television and told his son, "Okay, son, you can run along now while us men chat."

"But I thought you always wanted me to sit in on your—"

"Harvey!" Orville said, pointing to the door. "Close it on your way out!"

Pouting, Harvey rose to his feet and slouched his way out of the living room, with Brutus trotting behind him. Once the two men were alone, Porzinski finished his drink, then licked his lips.

"Mr. Peterjohn . . ." When Orville wagged a reproachful finger, he began again. "Orville . . . Let me assure you I intend to examine that son-of-a-bitch Cessna with a fine-tooth comb. And when I'm through, I'll have him nailed on violations that haven't even been invented yet!"

Orville held his cigar out and inspected it idly, then let his eyes shift casually over to the tax man as he said, "Actually, Phil, if I were you, Cessna Senior wouldn't be the one I'd investigate. . . ."

"Come again?" Porzinski said with a frown. "I don't follow you. . . ."

Raising the pitcher, Orville smiled at Porzinski, tilting his eyebrows suggestively. "Another martini, Phil . . . ?"

Twenty-six

Two weeks later, the Cessna family was paid a visit by a delivery man from United Parcel Service, who presented them with a huge, weighty box addressed to Kidco.

"It's from the television people!" Dickie shouted excitedly as he watched June cut the tape sealing the box. The rest of the family gathered in the living room and watched suspensefully.

"Oh my God!" June gasped once she'd opened the box.

"What!?" Bette cried out, straining to look. "What is it?"

June handed her sister the cover letter that came with the parcel, then upended the box, spilling several hundred envelopes and postcards out onto the table.

"I don't believe it!" Mrs. Cessna said, eyeing the deluge.

"Hey!" Dickie called out to Bette, who was skimming silently through the cover letter. "Read that out loud!"

"'. . . the enclosed letters and cards represent the greatest viewer response in the four-year history of *Kids Are the Darnedest People*'!"

"Whoopee!!" NeNe cheered as she joined the others in digging into the heap of mail.

"Careful with the return addresses," Mr. Cessna advised them, standing near the sofa with his wife, a prideful smile on his face. "If these kids took the time to write you, you can take the time to write them back."

His words fell on somewhat deaf ears, however, as the kids tore into the correspondence as if they were shucking off gift wrap on Christmas morning. Mrs. Cessna put an arm around her husband as they watched the children.

"Listen to this!" Dickie exclaimed, reading from one of the letters. "'I am ten years old and the newly elected president of the Dickie Cessna Fan Club, Cleveland Heights, Ohio chapter! Dickie, could you please send us an autographed picture . . . and a lock of your hair!'"

"What?" Mrs. Cessna said with amazement.

"I got a marriage proposal!" NeNe squealed, waving a letter in the air. Noticing something else in the envelope, she added, "He sent me his picture, too!"

When she took a look at the photograph, NeNe's eyes bulged outward and one hand went reflexively to her mouth to stifle a cry of shock. Seeing her reaction, Bette leaned over for a peek.

"What a banana!" she said.

"Let me see that," Mrs. Cessna said, breaking away from her husband and snatching the snapshot from her daughters. Doing a quick double take, her eyes widened with outrage. Mr. Cessna saw the reason for all the commotion and quickly tore the picture into shreds, much to NeNe's chagrin.

"He was too old for me anyway," she philosophized.

Meanwhile, Dickie was hoarding the lion's share of the correspondence, gloating as he read, "'Dickie'... 'Dickie Cessna'... 'Dickie'! Looks like I'm the people's choice!"

"No wonder, you little big mouth," June taunted vindictively. "You hogged the whole interview."

"Yeah, Dickie," Bette complained. "'President and Founder'... I thought we all found Kidco!"

"Come on," Dickie said, waving away their protests. "You two didn't even wanna be in it at first!"

"We're in it now, you creep!" June retorted. "And we work just as hard as you do!"

"Yeah!" Bette said.

"Now, kids..." Mr. Cessna said, trying to play the peacemaker.

Holding up his wealth of fan letters, Dickie made his case. "The public's never wrong, girls."

Before the quarrel could escalate any further, they were interrupted by the chiming of the front doorbell.

"Maybe it's my fiancé," NeNe quipped, heading for the door.

"I'll get it," Mr. Cessna said, holding his daughter back and telling the others, "You guys take it easy, okay? This isn't a war zone."

"Don't worry about me," Dickie said happily. "I've got two days of reading here...."

As the three girls resumed their harassment of Dickie, ignoring their mother's attempts to keep the peace, Mr. Cessna crossed the room to the foyer and opened the door.

Standing on the front porch were Phil Porzinski and his partner, Mel Sloman.

"I'm back," Porzinski said with false cheer.

Mr. Cessna sighed, stepping back and gesturing for the men to come in. Sloman nodded a polite hello while Porzinski looked around, taking in the spacious interior.

"Nice house you have here," Porzinski said. "Saw it on television Sunday before last...."

"All right, Porzinski, my kids played a prank," Mr. Cessna confessed. "I don't really live in a stable. That still doesn't mean I owe you tax on a sale made outside California."

"At the moment you made that sale, those horses were drinking from the river," Porzinski said, referring to a business transaction from a few months ago that had turned into a bone of contention between Mr. Cessna and the State Tax Board. "That means their heads were in California."

"But their *legs* were in Arizona," Mr. Cessna contended. "And four legs are bigger than one head!"

"Cessna," Porzinski said, grinning sadistically. "Let's forget about it for now."

"What?"

"We've got bigger fish to fry," Porzinski announced, striding past Mr. Cessna into the living room. Smiling at the children, he said, "Well, well. Long time, no see!"

Presented with a common foe, the children forsook their differences for the moment and offered a greeting of bleak acknowledgment to the tax men.

"How convenient," Porzinski said. "It looks like I've got the whole executive board together. Good! We have a few matters to settle concerning your tax situation, if you know what I mean. . . ."

The kids fell silent in the face of such prospects, leaving Mrs. Cessna to speak for them. "But the children were intending to pay income tax! It's too early for them—"

"This is *sales* tax, Mrs. Cessna," Sloman informed her, taking a less hard-line than his partner. "It's supposed to be collected on every sale and paid quarterly."

"And they've been selling manure for the last two quarters," Porzinski said, referring to his notes. "They owe the state six percent sales tax, *plus* interest and penalties for late payment."

"Penalties?" Mrs. Cessna questioned.

"Hey!" Dickie blurted out. "We're just kids!"

"Do you have a seller's permit?" Porzinski said with all the glee of a mad inquisitor.

"A what?" Dickie said.

"If you don't, it's a misdemeanor," Porzinski told him and his sisters. "That'll be another penalty, not to mention an injunction against any further sales until you get one."

The barrage of legal jargon carried an ominous tone on its own. Backed by Porzinski's ruthless delivery, the news came across to the kids like a charge of treason, punishable by death. Their father saw the terror in their eyes and stepped forward to intervene on their behalf, shouting, "For God's sake, Porzinski! These are children!"

"They're also a corporation," Porzinski said with finality, "and they're operating in violation of state law!"

As Sloman stood by, obviously uncomfortable with his partner's hard-lining, Porzinski reached into his suitcoat pocket and withdrew a document, which he unfolded and handed to Mr. Cessna.

"What the hell's this?" Mr. Cessna demanded.

"A court order for all Kidco's records," Porzinski said.

"What?" NeNe wailed, staring defiantly at the tax men. "You ain't taking my albums!"

"These are a different kind of records, NeNe," Mr. Cessna told her gently as he scanned the order.

"What's it mean?" June asked her father.

"I'm afraid it means you guys are going to have to take these gentlemen over to your office and let them have a look around."

With great reluctance, the Cessna children complied and accompanied Sloman and Porzinski the short distance to the stables. They'd recently put up a new sign proclaiming that the enclosure was NOW KIDCO LTD. VENTURES—WORLD HEADQUARTERS. Inside the upstairs office, a major renovation had taken place. A dividing wall had been put up to separate the stored clutter from the rest of the area, which was tastefully decorated and adorned with a few new additions that reflected the rising fortunes of the company. A sales graph showed the upward movement of Kidco profits, and a file cabinet next to the rolltop desk was filled with business-related documents that Porzinski began sorting through with blatant relish, while Sloman busied himself with admiring the television, video game and popcorn machines the children had installed in the office to help balance their workload with measures of recreation. The kids watched Porzinski gather together the information he was looking for, all of them uncharacteristically silent. Down below, the horses stirred noisily.

"Well, I think this will give us enough to work with for the time being," Prozinski finally announced, closing the near-emptied file cabinet and handing a portion of the appropriated bookwork to Sloman. As he was about to head for the ladder, he glanced down, spotting a stray sheet lying on the floor.

"Mel, that paper's got writing on it. Better grab it!"

Dickie beat Sloman to the sheet, snapping, "Those are my Pac-Man scores!"

"Is there anything else?" Porzinski asked the kids.

"Looks to me like you have it all," Bette said glumly.

"Are you sure?" the tax man asked.

Mr. Cessna had entered the office during the exchange, and he strode over with fierce certainty, placing himself between the tax men and his children.

"Porzinski," he said. "You better get out of here."

Porzinski met Mr. Cessna's gaze evenly. He was about to say something, but thought better of it and motioned for Sloman to give him a hand getting down the ladder with the expropriated documents.

"Sorry it had to happen like this," Sloman offered regretfully before joining his partner.

"Yeah, yeah," Dickie grumbled despondently. "You're just doing your job, right?"

"I'm afraid so," Sloman said.

"Mel..." Porzinski called from the top of the ladder.

As Sloman nodded a terse farewell and walked off, NeNe made a sour face, plopping into the couch along the far wall. Looking at her brother, she shook her head bitterly and said, "We always get caught...."

Twenty-seven

Harvey Peterjohn was the first one out of school when the last bell of the day rang, and he raced home with a giddy joy he hadn't felt since the last time he'd successfully copied a classmate's test paper without getting caught. He was so swept up by his rapture that he nearly ran past the entrance to the park without noticing his mother's car parked near the picnic area. He slowed down, catching his breath as he started over. When he was less than a dozen yards away, he opened his mouth, ready to call out, then suddenly fell quiet and ducked behind the cover of the nearest bush.

Mrs. Peterjohn was talking with another man at one of the picnic tables!

The man's back was turned to Harvey and his mother hadn't seen him yet, so Harvey carefully crept forward, staying hidden until he was within earshot of the conversation taking place at the picnic table.

"He *what*?" Mrs. Peterjohn whispered loudly.

"You heard me," the man answered. "He's on to you. I should know . . ."

"But . . . but, what's he on to me about? I don't understand any of this!"

"Of course you do. Don't play dumb!"

By now Harvey had inched his way to the far side of his mother's car, and he peered around the front fender for a better look. His mother was a prim-looking woman in her late forties, stylishly dressed except for a grotesque-looking hat that looked like a mutant carpet remnant. Craning his neck, Harvey leaned outward until he was finally able to get a good look at the man. It was Howard Carpenter.

Trembling with excitement, Harvey quickly backtracked his way to the road, then hurried home, bursting into his father's office while Orville was talking on the phone.

"That's great, Phil," Orville was telling Porzinski as he glowered at his son's unannounced intrusion. "Glad to hear it's going well. . . ."

Eager to make up for his blunder, Harvey remembered the original reason he'd sped home so fast and reached to his back pocket, withdrawing the most recent issue of the *Ramona Day Bugle*. He quickly unfolded the paper and laid out the front page on his father's desk so that the headline could jump out at Orville.

KIDCO BUSTED!
Exclusive Interview by Neil Brody

Somewhat placated by the news, Orville smirked at his son, wrapping up his conversation with Porzinski. ". . . Not at all. It was my duty to alert you tax people. Those kids were giving fertilizer a bad name! . . . Okay, Phil. Talk to you soon. Bye now . . ."

As he hung up the phone, Orville reached into his humidor for a cigar, apparently in too good a mood to bother giving his son a hard time about barging in. Instead, he fingered the paper ring wrapped around the cigar, saying, "You know, Harvey, this is a great country, just as long as we remember the government's there to serve *us*. You got that?"

"Yes, Dad," Harvey said dutifully, wondering how he was going to go about breaking the other news.

Orville lit the cigar, then picked up the *Bugle* for a closer look at the front page story on Kidco. "So," he chuckled, "it's the talk of the schoolyard."

"Yeah," Harvey said, shifting nervously. "Dickie Cesspool finally got his."

Orville had to hold the paper at a distance for the small print to come into focus. His lips moved as he read over the article, then he spoke aloud as he reached the bottom of the page. "'It looks like Kidco, for the time being, will have to rely on profits from its gopher operation.' Hmmmmm. Well, we'll just have to see about that, now, won't we?"

"Uh, Dad, there's one more thing I think that you—"

"Aha!" Orville interrupted, waving a cloud of cigar smoke out of his face as he reached over and picked the phone up, then punched three digits, snickering to himself. "Harvey, you're about to learn a very important business principle. When you have your opponent on the ropes, you don't back off... you put him *out*!"

"Right, Dad," Harvey stammered, "but, uh, first I—"

"Yes," Orville said into the receiver once the operator answered. "In San Diego, I'd like the number for the field office of the State Department of Food and Agriculture... thank you, I'll wait...."

While the operator was finding the number, the study door flew open for the second time in the past few minutes, and Mrs. Peterjohn stormed up to her husband's desk, jolting the phone from his hand and slamming it down on the receiver.

"Let's talk!" she said. Turning to her son, she pointed to the door. "Harvey, go walk Brutus!"

"Yes, Mother," Harvey said meekly, melting his way toward the door. Once outside the study, though, he stayed close by, eavesdropping on the confrontation taking place on the other side of the door.

"Orville Peterjohn, what is the idea of having a private detective follow me around as if I were some sort of wanton adultress?!!"

"Maria, sweetest," Orville said calmly. "Whatever are you talking about?"

"I just spoke with Howard Carpenter not less than ten minutes ago," Maria shouted. "He told me everything. Why, of all the nerve!"

"You deny that you've been seeing another man, then?"

"No, I don't," Maria said. "But I'll have you know that the man I was seeing was a travel agent setting up an itinerary for that trip you always wanted to take with me to Germany. I was going to surprise you for our anniversary, you snake, but now I've a good mind to cancel the whole thing!"

"Maria, Maria," Orville said, moving around his desk and approaching his wife. She backed away from him, avoiding his touch.

"Keep away from me, you worm!" Maria said. "Go play with your fertilizer, where you'll be in your element!"

"Forgive me, my dearest. . . ."

"Ha!" Mrs. Peterjohn spun around and rushed out the door, catching Harvey before he could slip from view. "And you! What's this? You're turning into a snoop like your father, too? What on earth is the world coming to?"

Twenty-eight

Once he'd had a chance to calm the marital waters, Orville Peterjohn put through another call to the San Diego branch of the State Department of Food and Agriculture, providing the bureaucrat at the other end with enough background information on the Kidco Goofer Gopher Killer enterprise to warrant sicking a field officer on the Cessnas. The job fell to Charles J. Grundy, a withered, dowdy soul with a penchant for drab suits, thin ties, and talking in a lifeless monotone. Like the tax men, he arrived on the Cessnas' doorstep with papers authorizing him to raid the Kidco makeshift laboratory in the equestrian stables. The family followed Grundy and watched as he began to dismantle various tubes, beakers and other paraphernalia that had gone into the making of the kids' homestyle pesticide.

"We're ruined," NeNe said glumly.

Struck down before our prime," Dickie elaborated.

"Lynched by red tape," Bette muttered.

"I'm afraid it won't do to plead your case with me, you youngsters," Grundy told them as he packed away the labels for the Kidco cans.

Mr. Cessna said, "It's not your department, right? You're just the guy who squints at the small print until you can track down some petty violation to slap against—"

"Actually," Grundy interrupted, holding up one of the filled cans, "we're talking about *several* violations, Mr. Cessna. First, the contents of this so-called 'Goofer Gopher Killer' must be listed on the containers itself, and must be listed with the Department."

"But that's our secret!" Dickie protested.

Shaking his head stuffily, Grundy told Dickie, "In the matter of pesticides, there are no secrets from the Department of Food and Agriculture, young man!"

"Mr. President to you, pal," Dickie retorted testily.

"Dickie!" Mr. Cessna scolded. "Go ahead, Mr. Grundy. . . ."

"They're also killing gophers for hire without a pest control license, which is a misdemeanor," Grundy advised. "They could be fined fifty to five hundred dollars for each offense . . . and/or imprisoned from ten days to six months."

"What?" June gasped.

"You can't be serious!" Mrs. Cessna exclaimed.

NeNe looked at her brother fearfully. "They want to throw us in the slammer!"

"Please," Grundy groaned, wincing at the barrage. "The Department only asks that Kidco cease and desist the exter—"

"Huh?" Bette said.

Simplifying his remarks, Grundy continued, "We want you to stop killing gophers, until such time as Kidco reveals the contents of its pesticide and its members pass the state examination for a pest control license. Now, I've brought along the material on which the examination's based. . . ."

Grundy opened his weathered attaché case and pulled out several thick pamphlets, passing them to the children.

NeNe perused the title of one, struggling with the advanced vocabulary.

"'Prin-ci-ples and . . . concepts of . . .' What's this next word? 'Very bratty'?"

"'Vertebrate pest control'," Mr. Cessna read over his daughter's shoulder. He took the pamphlet from NeNe and began thumbing through the pages, sampling the text while Grundy busied himself removing more cans of gopher killer from a nearby storage bin.

"Grundy, this looks pretty formidable," Mr. Cessna said dubiously. "'Anticoagulant baits' . . . 'Acute rodenticides' . . . How the hell do you expect children to pass a test based on this?"

"We don't, actually," Grundy said, a whiff of smugness in his voice. "It's our policy not to grant licenses to minors."

"Oh, that's great!" Mrs. Cessna said cynically. "Are you telling us the kids have to take a test they can't pass to get a license; and even if they could pass it you wouldn't give them a license anyway because they're under eighteen?!"

"Mrs. Cessna, please," Grundy implored, at the end of his limited patience. "I don't make the laws; I just enforce them. . . ."

With that, Grundy moved over and grabbed the handle of the next storage bin.

"No, not the oats!" Mr. Cessna shouted, rushing over. He was too late to stop Grundy, however, and the field officer yanked open the door, unleashing a torrent of oats that deluged him with such force that he was brought to his knees.

"Help!" Grundy howled, flailing his arms like a drowning man as the outpouring of feed swirled about him. Mr. Cessna finally managed to close the door to the bin, then reached over and helped Grundy from the floor.

"Sorry about that," Mr. Cessna apologized.

"I'm sure you are," Grundy said huffily, glaring at the family as he shook stray oats out of his cuffs and pockets. Dickie had to look the other way to hide his smile, and both NeNe and Bette were hard-pressed to contain their snickers.

"Serves you right," June told the inspector. "The way you come in here trying to spoil everything we've worked so hard for."

"Don't blame me, young lady," Grundy told her. "You

should have looked into the proper procedures before you involved yourselves in this misbegotten venture!"

"We were just getting rid of pests!" Dickie said. "We were doing everybody around here a favor, and now you're gonna let the gophers take over the whole town again! It's not fair!"

"My concern is with what's legal," Grundy said, wiping oats off his attaché case. "There're reasons for laws, you realize."

"Yeah." Dickie sneered. "They're there so guys like you have something to do, that's all."

Once he'd cleaned himself sufficiently, Grundy started for the door, dragging behind him the handcart loaded with the items he'd taken during his raid. Before leaving the stables, he looked back at the Cessnas and warned. "You haven't seen the last of me! You can count on that!"

"We were afraid of that," Dickie mumbled.

Twenty-nine

To say that the wind had been knocked out of Kidco's sails, not to mention their sales, would be more than a mere understatement. Like a boxer who'd just taken a hard right hook and an equally brutal left jab, the corporation had been felled and was in danger of not being able to get back on its feet. As the output of fertilizer dwindled, so did the spirits of the children, and without the authorization to produce more of their private stock of rodenticide, they felt that the gopher population of Ramona was proliferating at its greatest rate in history, almost as if the pesky burrowers were out to avenge their losses during the few weeks that Kidco Goofer Gopher Killer had been on the market.

By the end of the month, when the Cessna children convened at their headquarters to assess their situation, there was a cloud of gloom and despair hanging over their heads. As they went through the listless motions of a routine meeting, Dickie took up his position next to the sales graph, uncapping a Magic Marker while June read the treasurer's report, confirming everyone's worst fears.

". . . So, in a nutshell," June announced grimly, "our projected gross income for October is . . . zilch."

Taking the marker to the sales graph, Dickie drew a line straight down from the heights of their earlier success, making the line on the chart look like a mountain with a sheer cliff facing. Overcome by his frustration, he hurled the marker across the room, then sat down miserably on the rolltop desk. "Anything else?" he asked his older sister.

"Yeah, threats," June said bitterly, telling the others what they already knew. "If we break the cease and desist order on our gopher operation, the Department of Food and Agriculture says they'll take us to court. And if we don't pay our penalties by November first, the Board of Taxation says they will, too!"

Bette threw her hands up, crying, "If we pay them everything we owe them, we'll have to declare bankruptcy!"

Trying to be strong and calm in the face of tragedy, NeNe asked hopefully, "Think we can qualify for food stamps?"

Her question went unanswered as the others lapsed into a lingering, brooding silence. Dickie had his feet on his chair so that he could fold his arms across his knees. He stared disconsolately at his crumbling empire, feeling worse by the second.

"What do you think we should do, Dickie?" Bette asked him.

Instead of replying, Dickie lowered his head into the cradle of his folded arms.

"Dickie?" Bette repeated, concerned.

"I don't know!" Dickie cried out, looking up with teary eyes at his sisters, a broken boy. "The whole thing's falling apart! The government's after us . . . we can't make any money any more . . ." He jumped down from the table and began pacing. "You were right a long time ago, Bette. Childish, two-bit stunts! That's all Kidco is. . . ."

He slumped into the nearest armchair, languishing in his sorrow. The girls looked at one another, not sure what to do. Bette finally rose to her feet and slowly walked over to her brother, telling him softly, "Dickie. I said that about all the *other* stuff you did. Not Kidco."

Tears still streaming down his face, Dickie looked up at Bette uncertainly.

"As a matter of fact," Bette went on, "Kidco's the best thing I've ever been a part of."

"Me, too, Dickie," June called out from across the room.

"I liked the keno game better," NeNe confessed, "but they always caught us."

Dickie blinked his eyes and began rubbing away the tears on his cheeks. "But Kidco's kaput," he sniffed. "Finished . . ."

"No way, Dickie." Bette reached over to where the kids' first contract with San Diego Country Estates was posted on the wall. Taking down the framed document, she showed it to her brother, pointing out one of the clauses. "This says, 'unless Kidco screws up'. It doesn't say anything about *giving* up . . . and I don't think we should!"

June stepped over to her sister's side and smiled down at Dickie, whispering, "Me neither!"

"Me either, too!" NeNe chipped in, making it unanimous.

The show of faith was like a tonic for Dickie. He stayed where he was a moment, taking it all in, letting the affirmation drown his depression. Slowly the glint of determination flickered to life in his eyes, and the sulking tilt of his mouth gave way to a jaw that was clenched with new resolve. Finally he bolted from his seat, shouting, "You're right! Who do these dumb butts think they're pushing around?!"

"That's the spirit!" Bette said.

Dickie threw his arms around his sisters, blubbering, "Jeez, I don't know what I'd do without you three!"

"Oh, is that so?" June snickered sarcastically.

As they broke from their huddle and Dickie saw the looks in his sisters' eyes, he realized the point June had been trying to make. Mustering a show of humility, he told them, "I, uh, guess I got a little carried away lately. I mean, the TV show, and the letters and all. . . ."

"Yes . . . ?" Bette teased. "What about it?"

"Well, you know what an obsession is?" Dickie said, trying to recollect the brief lecture his father had given him a few months back. "It's like when you get so wrapped up in one thing that, well, how can I put it . . . ?"

"You become a royal pain in the ass?" June suggested.

"Yeah," Dickie conceded. "Something like that. Anyway,

I apologize to all three of you, and I promise it won't happen again!"

The girls conferred with a trading of glances, then Bette told Dickie, "All right, apology accepted!"

"Good enough!" Dickie said, becoming increasingly enthusiastic. "So, are we gonna stick together and fight!?"

"Of course!" June said.

"With our last ounce of manure!" Bette promised.

Thirty

The children were ready to fight, which was fortunate, since it came to pass that several weeks later they found themselves in court, squaring off against their bureaucratic adversaries. Although Phil Porzinski and Charles Grundy were on hand to lend moral support to the prosecution, the actual legal representative for California was State Attorney George Tuskie, a blue-suited, charismatic man in his late thirties, who was serving in his current post as merely the next stepping stone on what he perceived to be an illustrious road to success with the White House in Washington, D.C. as the final destination. Tuskie was a fighter, a scrapper who liked to approach his court cases with the same ferocity of a gladiator of ancient times, taking the attitude that defeat was a fate worse than death. As he sat at the prosecution table, skimming through his notes before the opening of the trial, Tuskie glanced over at the Defendants and muttered to Porzinski, "Those poor little bastards! They'll never know what hit 'em!"

"Oh yes they will," Porzinski gloated. "I'll make sure to remind them. I've been waiting a long time for this."

Mel Sloman was also present at the prosecution table, but he was sitting off to one side, trying to put as much distance as he could between himself and his cohorts. He was still suffering qualms of conscience about the whole proceedings and couldn't help but wonder aloud, "I can't help but thinking this is a lot of overkill. Look at those kids! Like lambs being led to the slaughter. It just doesn't—"

"Mel," Porzinski groaned at his partner, "bleed somewhere else for them, would you? You're making me sick."

"Yes," Grundy joined in, peering at Sloman over the tops of his bifocals. "This is a true showing of American justice, where all citizens are equal in the eyes of the law. It won't do to whimper about them being kids. They're corporate heads, pure and simple. . . ."

Sloman could only shake his head with resignation and inch his chair away from the others.

At the defense table, the four Cessna children sat nervously, properly dressed for the occasion. There were no other chairs at the table. Behind them, in the first row of the gallery, Mr. and Mrs. Cessna watched anxiously. Behind them, the rest of the seats were only partially filled. In addition to the usual court addicts and curiosity seekers, there was a knot of youngsters toward the back of the courtroom, whispering excitedly to one another as they pointed to the Cessnas. One of them was holding a handmade sign and waved it like a fan at a football game.

"Hey, look at that," Bette said, glancing back. "'Kidco Fan Club, San Diego Chapter.'"

"Lot of good a cheering section is going to do us," June whispered nervously.

"Come on, June, they're here to show their support," Dickie said, smiling over her shoulder and waving at the young clan. "It's nice to know there's people on our side, admit it."

"Yeah, well, if it was Perry Mason who was on our side I'd feel a whole lot better," June said.

"Is there a special prison for kids?" NeNe wanted to know, fidgeting in her chair.

"Oh, my God . . ." Bette gasped under her breath as she scanned the crowd and spotted Neil Brody sitting with a few other reporters in the press seats. He was jotting something down in his notebook, but when he glanced up and saw Bette looking at him, he grinned bashfully, tapping the rim of the fedora that made him look like a half-sized Walter Winchell.

"All right, all right," Dickie told his sisters. "Let's quit gawking around and start concentrating on our case, or we're gonna be goners!"

The bailiff, a stern-looking man with a powerful, commanding voice, banged a gavel for silence, then bellowed, "All rise!"

On cue, there was widespread shuffling throughout the courtroom as everyone rose to their feet. Most of them looked over toward the doorway closest to the judge's bench, which was yet to be occupied.

"Superior Court of the State of California for the County of San Diego is now in session," the bailiff intoned, staring vacantly into space as if he were merely coin-operated and had just been fed a quarter. "The Honorable Oliver T. Willoughby presiding. . . ."

The door to the judge's chamber opened, and Judge Willoughby walked purposefully to the bench and settled into his chair. He was an older man, with thin, silverish hair and tanned furrows creasing his brow. After taking in the assemblage before him with one quick, casual glance, he calmly said, "You may be seated. The clerk will read the information. . . ."

Once the crowd had sat down, the clerk, a shrewish looking man with slicked-back hair, held a sheet of paper and cleared his throat before reading, "The People versus the Corporate Officers of Kidco, Incorporated. The Defendants will please stand when called . . . Richard Cessna, Jr., President . . ."

As Dickie stood up, the members of the Kidco Fan Club cheered and applauded from the back of the courtroom, disrupting the proceedings. Dickie turned to acknowledge the ovation as Judge Willoughby reached for his gavel and pounded it several times to restore order.

"I'm pleased to see young people showing an interest in the judicial process," he told the members of the fan club patiently, "but let's remember, this is a trial, not a kickball game. Now, then, the clerk will proceed. . . ."

The clerk nodded his thanks to Judge Willoughby, then read, "Jeannine Cessna, Vice President; Bette Cessna, Secretary . . ."

"*Executive* Secretary," Bette corrected as she and NeNe rose to their feet next to Dickie.

The clerk rolled his eyes, then looked to make sure the court stenographer had noted the change before continuing, "June Cessna, Treasurer . . ."

June joined her brother and sisters in standing. They were all shaking slightly with nervousness, and NeNe stole a glance at her parents, who both nodded smilingly and gestured for her to keep her hopes up.

After taking in a deep breath, the clerk lowered the boom, reading, "The Defendants are charged with: Violation of the Revenue and Taxation Code of the State of California, Article Two, Section 6071—operating a business without a sales permit; and Section 7151—failure to furnish a quarterly sales tax return . . ." As if that weren't enough, the clerk came up for air, then dived once more into the sea of legal jargon, resuming, "And, with violation of the Food and Agricultural Code of the State of California, Article Two, Section 11702—pest extermination without a pest control license; and Section 12821—failure to list ingredients contained in pesticide."

This pronouncement raised a momentary stir in the courtroom, during which time NeNe leaned close to Bette and whispered, "How could we have done all that and still finished our homework on time?"

"Beats me," Bette grumbled, shrugging her shoulders.

"The Defendants may be seated," Judge Willoughby told the Cessna children. Then, glancing over at the Prosecution table, he asked, "Who is representing the People in this case?"

Tuskie rose to his feet, preening like an exotic beast in mating season, thumbs tucked in his vest pockets as he bounced lightly on the soles of his Florsheims. "George Tuskie, Your Honor," he introduced himself, turning in such a way that he could present his best profile to the media sketch artist. "From the Attorney General's staff."

"Mr. Tuskie," Judge Willoughby acknowledged with an almost imperceptible nod. Shifting his position, he looked over at the children, frowning. "And who's representing the Defendants?"

Dickie and Bette sprang up from their seats eagerly. Dickie spoke for them. "Me and Bette, Your Honor, and we object!" Pointing at Tuskie, he asserted, "That guy's only representing *some* of the people! A lotta *other* people are rooting for us!"

To prove Dickie's point, the Kidco Fan Club let forth with another volley of cheers and applause. Judge Willoughby reached for the gavel once more and banged it loudly, shouting, "We will have order in this court!"

Dickie and Bette turned around, motioning with their hands for the other youngsters in the gallery to comply. As an unsteady silence crept back into the courtroom, Tuskie took a step toward the bench.

"Your Honor," he said, "The Prosecution urges the court to overrule the Defendants' intention to serve as their own counsel. It would render these proceedings farcical."

"I object!" Dickie cried out. "What does 'farcical' mean?"

Judge Willoughby raised his hand to his head, lightly massaging his temples with the tips of his fingers in hope of warding off the migraine he felt coming on. As patiently as possible, he looked at Bette and Dickie. "Will the proposed counsel for the defense please approach the bench?" To make sure they knew what he was talking about, he curled his forefinger, gesturing for them to come over.

"Yes, Judge?" Dickie asked once he and Bette were standing on their tiptoes at the edge of the bench, peering up at Willoughby.

"It's my duty to warn you of the possible negative consequences of you representing yourselves," he told them. "Do you know what 'negative consequences' means?"

"It could be a bad idea?" Dickie guessed.

"That's right," Willoughby confirmed. "There's an old saying: 'Any man who represents himself in court has a fool for a client.'"

Dickie looked at his sister a moment. When it was clear that she didn't know what the judge was getting at either, Dickie stared back at Willoughby and said, "No offense, Your Honor, but if we believed in old sayings, we never would have made a penny! 'Youth is wasted on the young.' 'Children should be seen but not heard.' They all sound like they were made up by some old fart who hated kids!"

Judge Willoughby jerked back involuntarily at Dickie's candor, then coughed lightly as he brought himself under control. "Be that as it may," he said, "a licensed lawyer still has the advantage of seven years of training; four in college and three in law school...."

"That's okay, Your Honor," Bette told the judge. "We already sold manure and killed gophers without a license; we might as well do this without one, too."

"Besides," Dickie added, "us kids could never trust anybody who'd go to school an extra seven years *on purpose*!"

Willoughby started massaging his temples again as he waved the children back to their table. He wasn't sure who was responsible for assigning this case to him, but was determined to get even with whoever it was. Once his temples had been soothed enough for him to continue, the judge addressed the entire courtroom. "The Supreme Court has been quite liberal on people's rights to defend themselves. It's only required that they be literate. . . ." Training his stare on the Defendants, he said, "I assume you're both literate . . . you can read and write, can't you?"

"Your Honor," Dickie replied, slightly annoyed. "I know we're kids, but give us a break . . . !"

"All right, then," Judge Willoughby said over the light twittering that ran through the gallery. "All requirements having been met, we'll move right along—"

"Objection, Your Honor!" Tuskie said, lunging to his feet.

"On what grounds, Counselor?" Judge Willoughby asked.

"Well . . . it . . ." Tuskie fumbled for an explanation that could best express his irritation. The best he could come up with was, "It'll be plain silly!"

"I'll risk silliness, Mr. Tuskie, to guarantee these Defendants their rights," the judge said, overruling Tuskie's objection. Raising his voice another octave, he proclaimed, "The court accepts Richard Cessna, Jr. and Bette Cessna as co-counsel for the defense. . . ."

The San Diego Chapter of the Kidco Fan Club rose to its collective feet and greeted the judge's remarks with still another of their boisterous acclamations. Judge Willoughby had reached his bounds of endurance. Banging the gavel loudly as he stood up, he exhorted, "The court cannot accept these outbursts from the gallery! Bailiff, let's clear those noisemakers out of here. . . ."

As the bailiff and a few other uniformed officials made their way to the back of the courtroom to evict them, the youngsters booed the judge's decision. While they filed out, some of them shouted a few parting words of encouragement to the Cessna children.

When the bailiff opened the courtroom doors to escort the rambunctious youths, a dozen more kids swarmed past the startled official and headed for the seats, waving a placard that identified them as the Escondido Chapter of the Kidco Fan Club.

Judge Willoughby groaned audibly. It was going to be a long day.

Thirty-one

The first witness called to the stand was Charles Grundy. He was either wearing the same outfit as he had the day he'd first encountered the Cessnas or, more likely, he had a wardrobe filled with similar suits, shirts and ties. Grundy seemed like the sort of man who couldn't be bothered by such arbitrary decisions as choosing among radical differences in clothing styles.

As George Tuskie craftily led Grundy through his initial testimony, the Cessna children felt their spirits taking a beating. There was a certain shocking unreality to hearing themselves spoken about as if they were some modern-day version of the James Gang, flaunting lawless behavior in the face of all that was supposedly right and good with the world. Worse yet, Grundy had adopted a tone of benevolent righteousness, and was constantly looking at both the judge and the members of the press when he answered questions, doing a more-than-competent job of appearing like a decent, God-fearing man who was only seeing to his civic duty.

"So, Mr. Grundy," Tuskie said, wrapping up his questioning, "despite their flagrant violation of the code, you initially sought no criminal action against the officers of Kidco?"

"That's correct," Grundy explained humbly. "After all, they *are* children. . . ."

"But you changed your mind?" Tuskie asked.

Grundy hesitated, then slowly nodded his head, as if with great reluctance. "Yes. Last month, they resumed their pest control operation, still having failed to obtain a license, or to reveal the contents of their pesticide. They left us no choice."

As Grundy stared sadly at the children, NeNe and June quivered slightly, knowing that behind the inspector's facade of concern was a manic glee over the part he was playing in dealing a seemingly inevitable deathblow to Kidco.

"Thank you, Mr. Grundy," Tuskie said with a smile. Turning to Dickie and Bette, he gestured to the stand where Grundy was sitting and offered, "Your witness."

Like a triggered jack-in-the-box, Dickie popped to his feet, blurting, "We don't want him!"

As Dickie sat down, Judge Willoughby looked at him with disbelief. Elsewhere in the courtroom there was an undercurrent of murmuring as people mulled over the Defendants' tactics.

Not surprisingly, Tuskie bypassed Mel Sloman at first and asked Phil Porzinski to take the stand with regard to the initial testimony about Kidco's tax troubles. Unlike Grundy, Porzinski didn't bother with niceties. He scowled freely at the Cessna children as he answered Tuskie's introductory questions about the background of the case, and became increasingly haughty once he was asked to get into the specifics of Kidco's operations.

"To the best of your knowledge, Mr. Porzinski," Tuskie asked him, pausing before the witness stand, "what has been the extent of the children's business as far as selling fertilizer goes?"

"I think I have fairly accurate accounts here," Mr. Porzinski said, withdrawing a sheet of paper from his pocket. "Kidco's records list three hundred and forty-five sales of manure since March of this year."

"And they've paid tax on . . . ?"

"None of them," Porzinski said contemptuously.

There was sufficient whispered reaction in the gallery to send Judge Willoughby reaching for his gavel. He banged it until things were quiet, but refrained from having the Escondido branch of the Kidco Fan Club dismissed from the courtroom.

"Thank you, Mr. Porzinski," Tuskie said, striding back to the Prosecution table. Without even looking at his adversaries, he called out to Dickie and Bette, "Your witness."

Rising to his feet, Dickie declared, "We don't want *him*, either."

As Dickie sat down, his parents both cringed and leaned forward in their seats. Mr. Cessna whispered, "Dickie, do you know what you're doing?"

Turning around in his chair, Dickie whispered back, "Those guys have it in for us, so why should I talk to them?"

"Dickie, you're supposed to cross-examine them anyway and try to build up your case." Mr. Cessna was clearly having trouble keeping his promise not to intervene in the case.

"Okay," Dickie said. "I'll try to think of something."

Eventually it came Mel Sloman's turn to take the stand, and he did so with visible reticence. It was clear that he was taking no pleasure in his participation. George Tuskie knew it, too, and figured that would make him an even more credible witness in the eyes of the judge, especially when he substantiated Phil Porzinski's testimony right down the line.

"Just a few more questions," Tuskie said finally, noting his witness's discomfort. "Mr. Sloman, were the officers of Kidco advised that they were required by law to obtain a seller's permit if engaged in the sale of taxable items?"

"At what point do you mean? At first?"

"At any point," Tuskie clarified. "But particularly as far as two months ago, during your second encounter with them."

Sloman stared down at his lap, barely nodding his head.

"You'll have to speak up for the record, Mr. Sloman," Tuskie told him. "A nod doesn't translate very well into shorthand. Now, were the Defendants advised regarding their need to obtain a seller's permit at any point during their operations?"

"Yes," Sloman said raspily. "They were . . ."

"And did they obtain that permit?" Tuskie followed up immediately.

Sloman shook his head, then, before he could be castigated again by the Prosecutor, he muttered, "I'm . . . afraid they didn't. . . ."

"Thank you, Mr. Sloman." Tuskie beamed exultantly for the sketch artist as he stared at the children, again telling them, "Your witness."

This time Dickie wasn't so quick to his feet. He and Bette huddled their heads together, discussing strategy before Dickie finally stood up.

"Mr. Sloman," Dickie said earnestly. "Some of my baseball cards are missing, and Bette thinks you might have taken them by mistake when you cleaned out Kidco's records. If you find any, could you send them back to us, please?"

No one in the courtroom was expecting such a question, least of all Sloman. He stared at the youthful would-be attorney, trying to fathom the reason for his being asked about something so seemingly trivial.

"Pretty please?" Dickie said. "Ball cards are very hot commodities these days. They're part of Kidco's investment portfolio. . . ."

Sloman mouthed Dickie's last words silently, dumbfounded all the more. At last he was able to stammer, "Uh . . . well, sure . . ."

"Thank you," Dickie said crisply, dropping back into his seat. "No more questions, Your Honor."

Thirty-two

After a few Kidco clients were called to the stand to verify that both the manure and gopher-killing businesses were handled on a "cash only" basis, the prosecution ran out of witnesses. Since neither Dickie nor Bette called anyone else to the stand to speak on their behalf, the proceedings moved into closing arguments. It was late in the afternoon, and shifting shadows stretched across the courtroom. To NeNe they looked like prison bars, and she shuddered at the omen.

As Tuskie paced before the bench, allowing time for the dramatic tension to build, Dickie glanced over his shoulder, hoping to draw encouragement from the sight of the Kidco Fan Club. Instead, his eyes locked on Orville and Harvey Peterjohn, who were seated directly behind the prosecution table. Orville was absorbed with watching Tuskie carry out the final blows of his prosecution, but Harvey's gaze lingered on the Cessna children, and he leered vindictively at Dickie.

June looked back to see what had grabbed her brother's attention and whispered, "I bet that little creep Harvey's about ready to pee his pants from all the excitement."

"Yeah, well, he won't have long to wait," Dickie sighed with resignation, turning back to matters at hand. "We're goners. . . ."

"It's not over yet," June said hopefully.

"Don't count on it."

Tuskie looked over at the kids, holding onto the lapels of his jacket as he waited for them to fall silent. Once he was sure he had everyone's attention, he began speaking, directing his remarks to Judge Willoughby while he addressed the entire courtroom.

"Your Honor, the State's witnesses have confirmed not only the Defendants' violation of the law, but also a lack of repentance bordering on outright defiance!" Pointing an accusatory finger at the children, he invoked, "If these youthful miscreants—"

"I object!" Dickie shouted from his seat.

Annoyed at the disruption of his momentum, Tuskie dropped his hand to his side and glared at Dickie. Guessing the reason for the youth's outburst, he coldly said, " 'Transgressors?' "

Dickie looked at his sisters, who all shrugged their shoulders. "I still object," Dickie said.

"Troublemakers?" Tuskie offered.

"Okay," Dickie conceded. "We know that one."

There was a light snickering in the gallery. Tuskie rolled his eyes and paced a few steps, trying to regain the proper sense of righteous indignation in which to wrap up his remarks. When he was ready, he resumed, "If these youthful *troublemakers* are not punished for their actions, then we will all be guilty of encouraging flagrant disregard for the law among the wide-eyed children of this land." He let the words ring in the air a moment, then turned to Judge Willoughby and humbly mumbled, "Thank you, Your Honor."

As Tuskie returned to the prosecution table, there was a slight stirring in the gallery. One of the members of the Kidco Fan Club stretched a rubber band, took aim, and sent the projectile flying. Tuskie was grinning at Porzinski and just beginning to sit down when the rubber band slammed into the back of his head like a kamikaze mosquito.

"Yeeeeoooow!" Tuskie shouted, slapping at where he'd been struck.

"Mr. Tuskie?" Judge Willoughby inquired.

Tuskie whirled around in his seat, trying to spot the culprit who'd fired at him, but the entire fan club was sitting beatifically in the rear seats, like a choir of angels before the pearly gates. Turning back to face the judge, Tuskie said, "Nothing, Your Honor."

Judge Willoughby pivoted in his seat and faced the Cessna children. "Counselors, are you ready to present the case for the defense?"

NeNe leaned over and whispered hurriedly in Dickie's ear. Dickie stood up and relayed the message. "Yeah, Your Honor, but NeNe's gotta go to the bathroom. . . ."

"Real bad," NeNe pleaded, rising next to her brother.

"It's about time for evening recess, anyway," Judge Willoughby said wearily. Pounding his gavel, he proclaimed loudly, "Court will reconvene tomorrow morning at nine A.M."

As Judge Willoughby left the bench for his chambers, Porzinski patted Tuskie on the back, congratulating him. "Good job, George. You nailed those little tykes' butts, but good!"

"Well, I'd have to say it looks that way to me, too," Tuskie admitted with feigned modesty, filing papers back into his briefcase. Glancing over at the Cessnas, he shook his head pitifully. "I just wish they'd been smart enough to get someone with a little know-how to defend them. Makes me feel a little like the elephant gun being used to shoot sparrows."

"Ah, they deserve whatever they get," Porzinski said, turning to his partner. "Right, Sloman?"

Sloman rose from his seat and headed away from the table, muttering over his shoulder, "I'm going home. I'll see you in the morning."

"What's his problem?" Charles Grundy said. "Who's side is he on, anyway?"

"Not to worry," Porzinski said amiably. "He's one of those liberal types, that's all. Hey, how about supper together, boys? On me!"

"Can't turn down an offer like that," Tuskie said.

"Fine by me," Grundy said.

The three men rose from their table, casting one last glance at the defendants before excusing their way through the mass of Kidco fans crowding the gallery aisles, giving them vile stares.

"I can take a joke, whichever of you snots hit me with that rubber band," Tuskie said, "it just better not happen again, that's all I can say."

The fan club members gave the threesome an assortment of boos and raspberries, then continued making their way over to the Defendants' table, where they crowded around the Cessna children, asking for autographs and voicing their support. By now NeNe had left the courtroom, having made a beeline for the nearest restroom at the pounding of the judge's gavel.

"We're with you all the way!" one of the fans shouted.

"Yeah!" the others piped in.

"Thanks," Dickie said, trying to keep his chin up. "Now, if only we could get a jury trial and get all you guys on it, we might have a chance. . . ."

Thirty-three

"Kidco would like to welcome to this board meeting two distinguished guests who made it pretty clear we better invite them," Dickie announced, starting that evening's emergency session at Kidco's World Headquarters in the upstairs loft at the equestrian center stables. Acknowledging those guests, he said, "Mom. Dad."

Mr. and Mrs. Cessna were standing near the Kidco sales graph, which indicated that October's business had been greater than originally predicted, although question marks were scrawled in the column projecting the forthcoming month. They nodded at their children, trying to make their imposition as limited as possible.

"Okay," Dickie forged on. "First order of business. What are we gonna ask our witnesses?"

"Dickie," Mrs. Cessna said worriedly. "You *still* don't know that?"

Trying to sound unconcerned, Dickie bragged, "Mom, when I had to give an oral report on *The Last of the Mohicans*, I didn't even read it, and I still got a B plus!"

"And you're boasting about it?" Mrs. Cessna said. "That's terrible!"

"We're talking about something with greater repercussions than the outcome of an English report, Dickie," his father told him. Scanning the faces of his other children as well, Mr. Cessna went on, "Kids. I've told you before, I *do* know a couple of experienced lawyers, and they'd be glad to lend you a hand. . . ."

"But they aren't kids, Dad!" Dickie quickly countered. "*We* got ourselves into this, and we don't want to go running to grown-ups now to get us out! That's what Kidco's all about."

"That's a very nice speech, Dickie, but don't you think you're trying to play both sides of the fence?" Mr. Cessna said.

"What do you mean, Dad?"

Mr. Cessna broke away from his wife's side and began pacing before his kids, demonstrating how his son undoubtedly picked up the same habit. "On the one hand, you all want to be treated the same as adults, but at the first sign of trouble, it seems like your first reaction is to complain that everything should be taken care of for you just because you're children. Do you see what I'm trying to tell you?"

NeNe thought it over, then hazarded a guess. "You mean we can't have our cake and our candy bars, too?"

"Something like that, NeNe," Mr. Cessna said. "I mean, you're all bright, charming kids, but you can't count on always being able to get what you want just by turning on the ol' charm."

"We work hard, Dad!" Bette protested. "We earned all that we made!"

"I'm not arguing that, Bette. It's just that almost *everyone* works hard for what they make, and they still have to pay taxes of some sort . . . at least most of them do. Now, if you don't *want* to pay taxes, at least not any more than you have to, you should try to get around it legally, not by just saying you're kids."

"I know what you're saying," Dickie said. "We gotta find ourselves some loopholes. . . ."

Mr. Cessna backed up to his wife's side, telling the children, "Well . . . just know what your options are, that's all that I'm saying. Speaking of which, I think I've said enough.

If you don't mind, your mother and I will let you finish your meeting on your own. We'll be back at the house if you need us."

"Good luck," Mrs. Cessna said, smiling. "We're proud of you all and we're behind you, no matter what, okay?"

"Thanks," Bette said from the couch.

"Don't worry," Dickie told his parents. "We'll think of something."

After Mr. and Mrs. Cessna had left, the kids beat their brains collectively for another hour, but were unable to strike upon any sure foundation upon which to stage their last-minute defense. Late as it was, they finally adjourned their meeting, deciding that they'd be better off going back to court after a full night's sleep. Hopefully, one of them might have a brainstorm in their dreams and give them an idea that would help them out of their dilemma.

Dickie found that he wasn't able to fall asleep, though. Even after he'd turned the lights out, he couldn't stop his mind from racing. Moonlight flooded into his room, throwing a pale light on the images of his financial heroes posted on the walls, but none of them seemed willing to impart the proper inspiration. As the minutes ticked into hours, he finally decided he was wasting his time lying about idly. Throwing on his clothes, he stole from his room and out of the house, making his way back to the stables. Up in the loft, he leafed through the copy of the state penal code he'd checked out of the library the week before, familiarizing himself with all the laws that related to Kidco's situation. If anything, the multisyllable words seemed more likely to put him to sleep than to shine any new light on their case.

Finally Dickie followed another of his father's habits and saddled up one of the horses, deciding that a ride out in the country might help put things into a better perspective. He quietly walked the horse out to the trails, then mounted and rode at a steady canter up into the hills, making his way by the light of the moon and shivering slightly from the chill in the air. As he reached the higher elevations, he paused to look back at Ramona, slumbering peacefully in the valley below, illuminated by a scattering of streetlights down the main road. *Today, Ramona; tomorrow the world*. He remembered that cocky forecast he'd made so many months ago. It seemed like a completely different time, far removed from his current quandary.

"What's the answer, Big Red?" Dickie asked his horse. "Maybe we just had it all wrong. Maybe we shouldn't have bothered trying to do all we did. If we stuck to kid's stuff, we never would have gotten into all this trouble."

Big Red snorted, clopping its front hoof impatiently on the ground.

"Tired of hearing me complain?" Dickie said, snapping the reins. "Okay, let's get back to the stables. I might as well try to get some sleep, then get ready to take my medicine."

As he rode back downhill, Dickie's mood continued to sink into self-pity. The fight had been knocked out of him, and he was ready to give it all up. As they returned to the stables and Dickie began removing Big Red's gear, he started to think of how he'd go about admitting his defeat to his sisters, then to the judge. He wasn't looking forward to it, but there didn't seem to be any other way out.

Before leaving the stall, Dickie strapped on Big Red's feedbag, then petted the horse's head as it began to munch on its morning ration of oats. "Atta boy," he whispered sadly. "Thanks for listening."

Turning to leave, Dickie promptly stepped into a freshly deposited mound of manure.

"Darn you, Big Red!" Dickie snapped, his mood shifting abruptly. "What's the big idea? You trying to add insult to . . . hey, wait a minute!"

Dickie slowly raised his soiled foot and stared at the manure clinging to the sole of his boot, then back at Big Red, who was chewing away contentedly.

"Of course!" Dickie exclaimed. "Why didn't I think of it before?!"

By now his face was alight with a fresh, unexpected surge of hope and anticipation. Dickie quickly rushed over to the ladder, scraping the last of the dung off his shoes before climbing up to the loft. Switching on the overhead lights, he slid into his chair before the rolltop desk and went back to the penal code, flipping frantically through the pages.

Two hours later, the sun was starting to rise, and Dickie was still at it. Truly obsessed, from the look on his face it was clear that he'd stumbled onto something very, very big. . . .

Thirty-four

The Hall of Justice overlooked an expansive courtyard landscaped with thriving clusters of camellia and azalea. Tall palms stood in neat lines like lean sentinels on either side, and the courthouse itself shone brightly in the morning sun, wearing its tiled dome with dignified aplomb. On the wide flight of concrete steps leading into the building, the media was out in full force. Neil Brody was there, along with the few reporters who'd shared the press section in the courtroom with him the day before. They were joined by not only representatives from other newspapers, but also television reporters. Microphones and minicams were everywhere, crowding the steps with snakelike entwining cables.

The focus for all this attention had not yet arrived, but when a late-model Chevy Impala turned the corner and rolled to a stop near the curb in front of the courthouse, Neil Brody was the first reporter to spring into action. Knowing that the car belonged to the Cessnas, he hurried down the steps and rushed over, wriggling his way past the mingling crowd of spectators waiting for the courthouse to open.

"Dickie!" he called out to his fellow classmate as he stuck his head in through the opened rear window of the Impala.

Bette was sitting next to Dickie, and she batted her eyelids slightly as she smiled and said, "Hi, Neil . . . !"

The bug of romance had yet to bite Neil, and he failed to succumb to this advance as well. Ignoring Bette, he asked Dickie excitedly, "Have you seen the San Diego paper?!"

"We're in it?" Dickie said.

"In it?" Neil gasped, unable to control his enthusiasm as he grabbed the paper from under his arm and opened it for all to see. "You're on the front page!"

"Holy cow!" Dickie exclaimed, spotting the headline that dealt with yesterday's court proceedings. It read:

KIDS' FERTILE IDEAS DUMPED ON BY TAX MEN!

"Holy horse is more like it," June said, craning for a better look at the picture under the headline. "Oh, God, I look terrible there! My eyes are closed and that outfit—"

"Never mind that!" Dickie said. "We got the press on our side, that's what's important!"

"And it's only beginning," Neil explained, pointing over his shoulder at the other reporters and camera crews that were converging on the car. "They all want to interview you! One of them's from the network news!"

Dickie shot an eager glance at his sisters. NeNe threw open the front door and rushed out, howling, "Let's go!"

"All right!" Bette said, following her.

Dickie and June got out of the car simultaneously. He looked at his oldest sister, then moved close to her side and whispered, "June, stay away from the cameras!"

"Why?"

Dickie bobbed his head slightly, gesturing at her tight-fitting sweater. "We're supposed to be *kids*! We don't have bazongas like that!"

June glanced down at her chest, turning red with embarrassment. "'Bazongas'?" she mumbled.

It was too late for her to evade the Fourth Estate, though. Minicams were already whirring into life and still photographers were snapping pictures of the Cessna children with frantic haste. Seeing Bette flash a wide, cheerful smile, Dickie swept over to her side and advised, "Hey, tone it down! Don't look so happy! We're getting screwed, remember? Look like you're indignant. . . ."

"Excuse me, Dickie," a reporter shouted above his colleagues. "Is there anything you'd like to tell us before you go into the courtroom to wrap up the trial? What's your strategy?"

"If I told you," Dickie said firmly, "the bad guys might get wind of it and then we'd lose our advantage. So I gotta say 'no comment.'"

"Then you *do* have a plan?" the reporter questioned.

Staring over the man's shoulder at the photographer standing behind him, Dickie calmly asserted, "Of course I have a plan! Hang around inside and you'll find out all about it!"

A flurry of further questions fell on the children as they made their way through the throng of fans and reporters to the courthouse. Dickie extrapolated on a few generalities for the benefit of the reporter for the national news, but kept his planned defense a guarded secret.

Far above the congestion in the courtyard, an obese man in a pinstriped suit stood at the window of the judge's chamber, his teeth clamped around an unlit cigar as he stared down at the commotion. Sid Fein was in charge of Judge Willoughby's forthcoming reelection campaign and, from the look on his face, he was filled with reservations about the most recent turn in that campaign drive. Taking the cigar from his mouth, he turned from the window with disgust.

"Well, Ollie," he grumbled, walking over to where Judge Willoughby was sitting at his desk. "It looks like you're on TV tonight, and not in the sort of light we want you in."

"Tell me about it," the judge groaned, lowering the morning paper he'd been reading. "I'm already all over the morning edition. . . ."

"Ollie, you're all over *everywhere*!" Fein went over to the bookcase near the door and grabbed up the stack of other papers he'd brought in earlier that morning. "The damn story was picked up by the wire services, for crying out loud!"

"I *thought* I saw someone from Associated Press," Judge Willoughby recalled bleakly.

At random, Fein picked up various morning editions and read off the headlines with increasing irritation. " 'KIDCO SELLS THE MANURE, BUT STATE WANTS ITS OWN PILE' . . . that's from the Chicago *Tribune* . . . Here's *The New York Times* . . . 'GOVERNMENT SNIFFS AS KIDS PILE UP LOOT' . . . From the *Herald-Examiner* up in L.A. . . . 'RED TAPE PESTS TO EXTERMINATE KIDCO' "

"All right, I've heard enough," Judge Willoughby said.

"You can guess who the public's going to side with," Fein complained as he threw the papers back down on the bookcase and stuffed his cigar back in his mouth.

"Bad as it might look, I can't help it, Sid," the Judge said as he got up from his seat and started putting on his black robe. "You have to admit, Tuskie built up a pretty strong case yesterday."

"Ollie, aren't I making myself clear here?" Fein growled around his cigar. "You have to run for reelection, and who's going to vote for a man who sends four little kids up the river for *any* reason short of murder?"

"Sid," Judge Willoughby said, forcing a smile. "Come on, now. I know this isn't the best of publicity for me, but don't you think you're exaggerating, just a little?"

"Am I?" Fein said, snatching his cigar out of his mouth and snapping it in half. "That's what's going to happen to your chances if you make martyrs out of those kids. Remember what happened to the witch who tried to stick Hansel and Gretel in the oven?"

Judge Willoughby thought about it a moment as he straightened his robe and inspected himself in the full-length mirror behind his door. Finally he turned to Fein, a perplexed expression on his face. "You know, Sid . . . come to think of it, I *don't* remember what happened to that witch. . . ."

Thirty-five

When the trial resumed, the gallery was packed, mostly with reporters and children supporting Kidco. When Dickie asked if he could call a few witnesses to the stand before his final arguments, it didn't take long for Judge Willoughby to decide that he could bend the rules.

"Just this once, though," he admonished.

"Thank you, Your Honor," Dickie said. "I'd like to call to the stand my school principal, Mr. Ruggles. . . ."

Principal Ruggles stood and excused his way through the children surrounding him, then came down the aisle and was sworn in. He sat down nervously on the witness stand as Dickie began to pace before him, trying to refrain from showing how much of a thrill it was for him to be in a position where he could interrogate his principal.

"Mr. Ruggles," he finally asked, "how many times did you have me and Defendant NeNe sent to your office last year?"

"Well, that's quite a question," Mr. Ruggles laughed uncomfortably. Counting the incidents off on his fingers, he recollected, "Let me see . . . there was the football pool; the roulette table; wholesale cafeteria food; fire drill bingo; keno;

'We Forge Pink Slips'; 'Rent a Third Grader' . . . seven. There might be more, but that's all I can think of right now."

Dickie paused a moment, giving the press a chance to jot down all these various claims to notoreity, then asked Mr. Ruggles, "And how many times have we been sent to your office since we started Kidco?"

"None, I'm amazed to say," the principal admitted.

"And Kidco did a good job of taking care of the gophers that were tearing up your rose garden, didn't they?"

"Yes," Mr. Ruggles said, nodding his head for all to see. "Very good."

"Our pleasure," Dickie told him, grinning contentedly. Glancing over at Judge Willoughby, he said, "No more questions, Your Honor."

George Tuskie wasn't interested in cross-examining Mr. Ruggles, so the principal stepped down and the next witness was called. Jim Clark, proprietor of the San Diego Country Estates, took the stand and, sworn in, at Bette's request, divulged his position and the nature of his business relationship with the Cessna children.

"Mr. Clark," Bette followed up, "you've employed Kidco for a considerable time now. Would you say we've done a good job?"

"I sure as hell would," Clark affirmed instinctively. Then, seeing the look of displeasure on Judge Willoughby's face, he softened his answer. "Uh, yes. I would."

"Your Honor," Tuskie said with bland irritation, rising from his chair. "The prosecution objects to this whole line of testimony. Whether or not the officers of Kidco did a 'good job,' whether or not they get in less trouble at school—these aren't the issues that are being tried here."

"We think they are!" Dickie protested, bolting to his feet. As he made his way around the side of the defense table, Bette eased away from the witness stand.

"My co-counsel brother will handle that objection," she said on the way back to her seat.

"Your Honor," Dickie said, infusing his remarks with as much melodrama as he could. "We see kids getting in trouble all the time, and we see stories in the papers and on TV about all the juvenile delinquency. Who knows? If me and NeNe wouldn't have started Kidco, we might have kept up our evil ways and wound up in reform school! But we went straight, Your Honor, with the help of our loving sisters. . . ."

"Yeah!" June called out, spurring on a brief display of support from the kids in the gallery that was quickly met by a warning pound of Judge Willoughby's gavel.

Once the outburst had subsided, Dickie resumed, "Now we work hard, stay off the streets, and don't break any windows or do any of that stuff that real criminals do." Letting his voice rise to the point where it was about to crack with emotion, Dickie blinked away a few would-be tears as he indicated Tuskie and steamed, "This big jerk—"

"I object!" Tuskie shouted.

Ignoring the objection, Dickie went on, "This jerk says if we don't get punished for what we did it'll encourage other kids to break the law." When Judge Willoughby showed no signs of interrupting him, he poured on the pathos. "But what did we do? We're just kids, Your Honor, and instead of giving us trouble about taxes, the government ought to be glad we're out working on our own, setting a good example and not stealing any hubcaps. . . ."

"Your Honor," Tuskie interrupted, "I fail to see the point of this trite oration!"

Dickie countered, "What I fail to see the point of is making kids take a test they could never pass to get a pest control license they could never get anyway because they don't give them to kids!"

"Your Honor!" Tuskie demanded.

Judge Willoughby clutched at his gavel, but stopped short of pounding it. He could see the mood of the courtroom and could still remember his campaign manager's lecture earlier this morning. He slowly released the gavel and nodded for Dickie to continue.

Playing up to the press, Dickie said, "What's the point of asking us to give away our secret formula, when that would mean it wouldn't be a secret anymore, and everybody could make it up themselves and then they wouldn't need us!? Your Honor, if Kidco's put outta business on account of licenses and taxes and crummy laws, what about all the other kids? They'll figure doing a good job and staying out of trouble only gets you in *worse* trouble, and they'll just take a lotta drugs and become a bunch of bums! And then when they grow up, we'll have a nation of good-for-nothings, and I bet some foreign country'll come in and take over! And hundreds of years from now, people'll look back and say 'The United States was the greatest place in the world, and then they had to go and bust Kidco!'"

Out of breath, Dickie fell silent, but all around him the courtroom exploded into applause and cheering as the assembled fans rose to their feet and awarded him with a standing ovation. Even Jim Clark joined in from the witness stand. Dickie acknowledged the reception with a bashful smile, then slowly returned to the defense table. Before sitting down, he grinned at his parents in the front row and whispered, "Whew! That was even better than my *Last of the Mohicans* report!"

"You're something else, Dickie," Mrs. Cessna whispered back.

"Order!" Judge Willoughby was calling out above the hammering of his gavel. "Order, or the gallery will be cleared of all children but the Defendants! And I mean it!"

Once the ruckus dwindled to a manageable chorus of whispers, George Tuskie rose and complained, "Your Honor, you still haven't ruled on my objection. . . ."

"Quite right, Mr. Tuskie," Judge Willoughby replied. Looking over at Dickie, he said, "Counsel for the Defense will apologize to Counsel for the Prosecution for calling him a jerk."

"Your Honor, my *prior* objection," Tuskie said icily. "The testimony of the defense's witnesses, and this last little diatribe we've just suffered through, have absolutely no bearing on the charges brought before this court!"

"I see your point, Mr. Tuskie," Judge Willoughby conceded. He reflected a moment, then turned slightly, spotting Sid Fein waving to get his attention in the back of the courtroom. The fat man was pantomiming an eating gesture, then pointing at the wall clock. Taking the hint, Willoughby nodded and raised his gavel. "We'll take an extended noon recess," he announced. To appease Tuskie, he focused a stern gaze on the Cessna children and told them, "I encourage Counsel for the Defense to use this time to develop a line of questioning that will more directly address the issue of their innocence or guilt."

"Hallelujah," Tuskie muttered, slamming closed his briefcase.

At the defense table, Dickie nodded to Judge Willoughby, then whispered under his breath to his sisters, "Some people sure are picky. . . ."

Once the men at the prosecution table left the courtroom and reached the outer corridor, Tuskie and Charles Grundy headed for the nearest vacant anteroom while Porzinski and Sloman went to the row of phones lining the lobby wall. While Sloman put through a call to his wife, Porzinski lit up a cigarette and dialed Orville Peterjohn's number. Orville answered on the third ring.

"Hello?"

"Orville, it's Porzinski."

"Phil, how's things on the front? Sorry I couldn't make it down this morning, but I had some other matters to tend to."

"Well, I think we still have the goods on them, but those snotnoses are scraping up a few tricks from the bottom of the barrel."

"I'm not surprised. They're a nefarious group, all right. Especially that Dickie . . ."

"Right," Porzinski said, tapping ash onto the tiled floor of the lobby. "He shot his mouth off like he was God's gift, but no damage done. I'd say if you want to be here for the kill, it could be this afternoon."

"I wouldn't miss it for the world."

"Okay, Orville, see you soon."

Porzinski was smiling with satisfaction as he hung up the phone. When he turned around, Sloman was staring at him.

"Phil, I assume we're recommending leniency in this case."

"Don't make me laugh, Mel," Porzinski sneered. "How lenient was that little shit when he sent us all the way to Tijuana?"

"But that's such a petty thing, Phil. It's nothing—"

"It's everything!" Porzinski retorted. "My God, are you such a knee-jerk softie that you can listen to that kid blabber his harebrained platitudes without getting sick?"

"I guess maybe I can just remember my own childhood a little clearer than you can yours, Phil," Sloman said.

"Oh no, you don't," Porzinski groaned, heading for the nearest exit as he waved his arms. "Please, don't tell me about your Sunday drives in the fresh air and all that Goody Two-shoes crap. You'll ruin my appetite!"

"Mine's already ruined," Sloman said glumly, trudging out the door.

Thirty-six

As Mr. Cessna guarded the outside entrance to their anteroom, keeping out the insistent throng of reporters, the Cessna daughters sat around their mother, finishing their sack lunches. Dickie was over in the corner, debating with Neil Brody as they stood on either side of a large, swollen shopping bag.

"Neil, there must be a hundred kids out there!" Dickie told him. "Look, I'd take care of this myself, but I'm kinda busy today, if you know what I mean. . . ."

Neil pushed his glasses up on his nose and tried to hold his ground. "Dickie, I'm a journalist covering a trial! Who's gonna believe I'm objective if I start selling Kidco T-shirts?"

Wanting to settle things as quickly as possible, Dickie lifted the bulky bag and offered, "Look, Neil, they go for five dollars a shirt. We'll give you a twenty percent commission."

Neil was as good at math as he was at journalism. Realizing that he'd just been given an offer he couldn't refuse, he took the bag from Dickie, rationalizing, "I can always say I was working undercover. . . ."

When Neil opened the side door, the sounds of pandemonium poured in, and the children looked over to see the unruly waves of humanity crashing against the doorway being defended by their father and a uniformed officer. As Neil bent over and made his way past the human barricade to start hawking T-shirts, June's boyfriend wrangled his way past Mr. Cessna and into the room.

"Juney!" he called out.

Pointing at Frank, Dickie shouted to the officer, "Marshal . . . !"

But the door closed and Frank rushed over to June's side, where they embraced as passionately as they thought they could get away with in the presence of Mrs. Cessna.

"Frank!" June gasped.

"I had to be with you, Juney!" Frank whispered breathlessly. "Forget anything bad I've ever said about Kidco. I love you!"

Bette and NeNe smirked at one another at the sight of their sister's clinging to Frank.

"Spare us, please," NeNe said.

"How gross," Bette agreed, although she secretly envisioned herself sharing a similar embrace with Neil Brody.

"What about the money you owe me from last week, Frank?" Dickie demanded, moving over to the table. "I won't go easy on you like I did the first time. It'll be in three figures before you know it. . . ."

Throughout these various taunts, Frank and June maintained their embrace. Bette finished her sandwich, then stood up, in a huff. "Well, if she's gonna do that all day," she complained, "I'm gonna go help Neil . . . !"

Bette ran over to the door and yanked it open, unaware that her father had been leaning against it. He staggered off balance into the room as his daughter stormed past him.

"Bette, wait!" he called after her.

"Aw, let her go," Dickie told his father. "We're all done here."

"All done?" Mr. Cessna said once he'd managed to shut the door to drown out the clamor in the lobby. "What about your defense?"

Dickie shrugged his shoulders, trying to show his obvious disappointment. "There's nothing more we can do. The ace we had up our sleeve never showed up. . . ."

Mrs. Cessna looked over at her son and asked, "What ace? Who are you talking about, Dickie?"

Dickie sighed, "Mr. Woodward said he'd get here as soon as he could, but it looks like it's gonna be too late for him to help us."

"I don't get it," Mr. Cessna said. "How's Homer supposed to help you out, anyway?"

"It doesn't matter if he doesn't get here," Dickie said, looking at the clock as he grabbed his briefcase. "We gotta get back. It'll be hard enough throwing ourselves at the mercy of the court without showing up late to do it. . . ."

When they left the anteroom, the defendants filed through the spectators and reporters still lingering in the lobby, then took up their seats in the courtroom. As it turned out, Judge

Willoughby was a few minutes late, and the children had a chance to look over the audience behind them. Whatever consolation they felt in seeing a sprinkling of Kidco T-shirts being worn by ardent supporters was almost completely negated by the arrival of Orville and Harvey Peterjohn, who made their way down the center aisle with looks of joyous expectancy. There was still no trace of Homer Woodward.

Judge Willoughby entered the courtroom and settled into his chair, then said, "All right. Counsel for the Defense, the court trusts you heeded its advice during the recess. I hope you don't plan to disappoint us."

Dickie was only half-listening as he continued to scan the gallery. When Bette nudged him and whispered in his ear, Dickie whirled around and jumped to his feet.

"Yes, Your Honor," he said, fidgeting with a pen. "We, um, might need a little more time to . . . that is, we—"

"Psst, Dickie!" NeNe hissed, tugging the cuff of her brother's corduroy jacket. Once she had his attention, she gestured to the back doors leading into the courtroom, and Dickie looked to see the reason for NeNe's excitement. Homer Woodward was standing just inside the doors, having an argument with the officers who tried to tell him the gallery was already filled beyond capacity by children, reporters and curiosity seekers.

"Okay!" Dickie said, his confidence returning to him as he looked back at the judge. "If we have to prove we're innocent on top of everything else, we can do it! The defense calls Mr. Homer Woodward to the stand. . . ."

The announcement brought forth a few sniggers in the gallery. George Tuskie looked at Grundy and Porzinski questioningly, but neither of the officials had any idea who Woodward was. Orville Peterjohn did, but he couldn't understand the reason Dickie was calling him.

The clerk called out loudly, "Is Homer Woodward in the courtroom?"

Jerking his arm free from one of the restraining officers, Homer shouted, "Yup!"

"Take the stand, please," the clerk told him, trying to keep a straight face at the sight of the farmer, who was still wearing his coveralls and farm hat as he walked up the center aisle to the witness stand. When the clerk held out a bible,

Homer stared at it a moment, confused, then reached for it as if he were planning to read through it.

"No, sir, just put your left hand on the cover and raise your right," the clerk said stiffly. "Is that clear?"

"Yup."

"Do you swear to tell the truth, the whole truth, and nothing but the truth, so help you God?"

"Yup," Homer promised.

"Be seated," the clerk told him.

As Homer settled into the seat and stared out at the multitude watching him, Dickie came forward, ready to play his ace in the hole.

"Thanks for coming, Mr. Woodward," he told Homer. "Could you please tell everybody here if you own Woodward's Feed Store in Ramona?"

"Yup."

"Does my dad buy hay and oats and straw from your store?" Dickie asked.

"Yup," Homer answered, ever to the point.

"And does my dad pay sales tax on everything he buys from you?"

"Yup."

At the prosecution table, Porzinski was the first to guess what Dickie was getting at. By the time he nudged the attorney next to him, Tuskie had figured it out, too. "Your Honor," he said, rising. "No one is accusing the Defendants' father of failing to pay sales tax on horse feed. . . ."

"Good!" Dickie exclaimed. "Because all Kidco sells is straw composted with manure . . . which used to be hay and oats!"

A buzz of conversation began to filter through the gallery as Dickie veered over to the bench and appealed directly to Judge Willoughby. "Your Honor, even us kids know that if our dad pays tax on the stuff going into the horse, we shouldn't have to pay more tax on the *same* stuff coming back out! We'd be getting taxed on both ends!"

Dickie spun around and headed back to his seat. The gallery unleashed a spontaneous burst of renewed cheering, and his sisters slapped him pridefully on the back as he sat down. Across the way, the prosecution table was a scene of sudden frustration. Tuskie, Porzinski, and Grundy were all dazed by the implications of Homer's testimony. At the far end of the table, Sloman was trying hard not to smile.

Judge Willoughby looked over at his campaign manager, following Sid Fein's gestured advice and letting the ovation run on for a few seconds before putting his gavel to work and then moving in to close the case.

"Order! Order!" Once he had quiet, the judge observed, "Mr. Tuskie, the defense *does* make a strong argument that tax has already been collected on the item they're selling. Surely one of our State agencies doesn't seek to tax the same items *twice* . . . ?"

Tension hung in the air as Tuskie conferred with Porzinski, who began thrashing through his notes and files in a desperate attempt to salvage the prosecution's case. Sloman smiled freely now at the sight of his partner's irritation, then glanced over at the defense table, where the children were poised nervously, waiting to see what the outcome might be. The clerk took advantage of the lull to escort Homer from the witness stand.

"Mr. Tuskie . . ." Judge Willoughby called out impatiently.

Tuskie held up a hand without taking his eyes off the rustling papers he and Porzinski were going over.

"One moment, Your Honor," he pleaded.

"That won't be necessary," Mel Sloman suddenly said, standing up for the first time during the trial. Looking at the judge, he said, 'Your Honor, on behalf of the Board of Taxation . . . we made a mistake."

The outcry from the gallery this time was even louder. Children jumped up and down, shouting and clapping their hands. Reporters grinned to one another as they wrote it all down.

Over the sound of his pounding gavel, Judge Willoughby announced, "As the Board of Taxation acknowledges its error, the charges against Kidco are dismissed!"

"Whoooooopeeeeee!" NeNe screamed, bolting from her chair and rushing to throw her arms around her mother, who was leaning over in the front row behind them. June hugged Frank while Dickie and Bette both crowded into the enveloping arms of their ebullient father.

"I'm so proud of you guys!" he told his children.

"We did it! We did it!" Dickie and Bette enthused

simultaneously, offering victory smiles to the reporters crowding around them.

In the midst of the rampant celebration, Porzinski and Sloman began to argue, while Orville and Harvey Peterjohn sat rigidly in their seats behind the prosecution table, both stunned by the verdict that had been handed down.

"Dad, we lost!" Harvey whined, sounding as if such a possibility were impossible for a Peterjohn.

Orville wasn't in a whining mood, though. He was angry, and the more he thought about all that he'd invested into the events leading up to the trial, the madder he became. It didn't take long for an idea to pry its way through the boiling wrath. A manic grin crept across Orville's face as he snorted. "Those little bastards aren't all the way out of the woods *yet*!"

Leaning forward, Orville jabbed his forefinger into Charles Grundy's ribs, launching the bureaucrat to his feet. When Grundy turned around, Orville motioned him closer, then whispered something in his ear.

"But of course!" Grundy gasped, a hopeful spark coming to his lifeless eyes as he passed the message along to Tuskie, who reacted similarly.

"Your Honor!" Tuskie roared, standing still another time. "Your Honor!!!"

Willoughby banged the gavel like a carpenter working overtime before he was able to lower the din in the courtroom to a level he could speak over.

"Yes, Mr. Tuskie?"

With malicious certainty, Tuskie insisted, "The charges that the officers of Kidco failed to obtain a pest control license, and to reveal the contents of their pesticide, remain before this court!"

A communal groan washed over the gallery, and the disappointment was shared by the Cessna children, who reluctantly returned to their table.

"Bummer," NeNe mumbled, sitting down.

"You're, uh, quite right, of course, Counselor. . . ." Judge Willoughby stammered, not sure what step to take next. He looked to Sid Fein for a cue, and the fat man pointed over the judge's shoulder. Catching on, Judge Willoughby nodded, then said, "I'd like to see both Counsel for the Prosecution and Counsel for the Defense in my chambers. . . ."

Thirty-seven

"Okay, let's get right down to the core of this whole thing," Judge Willoughby said, staring over his desk at Dickie and Bette. Tuskie was still outside, having a last-minute discussion with his clients.

"What's that?" Dickie asked.

"Right now things are looking highly in your favor," Judge Willoughby explained. "The biggest obstacle you're going to have to face at this stage is that the State won't want to back down completely and end up with nothing but egg on its face."

"Hey, maybe somebody from our fan club shot a rubber band at Tuskie," Dickie said, "but they aren't going to start throwing eggs at him!"

"I was speaking figuratively," the judge said. "What I mean is, if you're willing to make some sort of concession on your part, this whole sorry episode will be done with, hopefully once and for all."

"What kind of concession?" Bette said.

Just then the door to the judge's chamber opened and George Tuskie entered. Much of the hardness was gone from his face, but there was still a glint of determination in his eyes.

"You'll find out shortly," Judge Willoughby whispered to the children, then gestured to a vacant chair and told Tuskie, "Have a seat, George."

Tuskie sat down across from the Cessna children, avoiding their gaze at first. An uncomfortable silence filled the room, then the attorney offered Dickie a grudging smile and said, "I have to admit, you pulled a nice one out there. Pulled our case out from right under our feet as far as the tax problems went."

"Thanks," Dickie said. "I, uh, I'm sorry about calling you a jerk. I guess I got a little carried away with myself."

"I've been called worse, let me assure you." Tuskie turned his attention to Judge Willoughby and sighed. "So, that leaves us with the matter of Kidco Goofer Gopher Killer. . . ."

"Precisely," Judge Willoughby said. "George, there must be *some* compromise we can work out."

"Well, Mr. Grundy has said he doesn't want his department to look too . . . heartless," Tuskie confided, his voice taking on an almost conciliatory tone. "He might be willing to grant Kidco a special permit until such time as the officers come of age. . . ."

"Oh yeah?" Dickie said, leaning forward in his seat. "That'd be great!"

"What about our secret formula?" Bette asked.

Tuskie mulled it over a moment, then suggested, "Perhaps it could remain a secret, under lock and key in the department's office."

"It wouldn't have to be on the can?" Dickie said.

"Probably not," Tuskie bargained. "But, of course, the prosecution would expect a little something in return for these concessions."

"What do you have in mind, George?" Judge Willoughby asked.

"A guilty plea on the two remaining counts," Tuskie said, "with the court's assurance they'll be fined for each offense."

"George, that's fifty dollars a gopher!" Judge Willoughby exclaimed.

Dickie gasped, "And we knocked off six hundred of 'em!"

Bette shook her head to herself as she multiplied the figures.

"Judge," Tuskie said, holding his ground. "Grundy doesn't want to get embarrassed by this case any more than you do, but the State's not coming out of it empty-handed!" Looking over at where Bette was grimacing at the total she'd come up with, Tuskie added, "Don't worry, we know their assets. They can afford it . . . just."

"I don't know . . ." Judge Willoughby said. "I was hoping for something less harsh."

"Well, there's no loophole on this matter," Tuskie reminded him. "We've got Kidco dead to rights, and it could be a whole lot worse for them. That deal's the best I can do, I'm afraid."

"I see." Judge Willoughby turned to the children. "Would Kidco be willing to accept this compromise?"

Dickie looked at the figures his sister had jotted down. Neither of them seemed enthralled with the option that had been laid out for them.

"I dunno, Judge," Dickie finally sighed. "We gotta talk it over with NeNe and June. . . ."

"I understand," Judge Willoughby told them. "I can give you until tomorrow morning to give me your answer. All right?"

Dickie nodded glumly. He and Bette rose from their seats and left the judge's chamber, reentering the courtroom, which was now vacant except for a janitor cleaning up the gallery floor.

"Well, one way or another, it looks like this is going to be the end of Kidco," Dickie said.

"Come on, Dickie, don't talk like that!" Bette countered, trying to remain optimistic. "Remember what they always tell you in Little League? It's not over until the last out."

"Yeah, well, we're in the big leagues, now," Dickie said. "And we're way behind in the bottom of the ninth, with two outs and two strikes against us. . . ."

Thirty-eight

Dickie's disillusionment had spread to the others by the end of the day, and when the Cessna family gathered together that evening in the corporate loft, there was a general feeling that it might well be the last official meeting of Kidco.

"So, when we're done paying the fine, provided it's fifty dollars for every gopher we exterminated," June said, consulting her business ledger, "we'll have a balance of . . . thirty-eight dollars."

"Not even ten bucks apiece," NeNe sulked.

"I feel like I'm headed for a Great Depression," Dickie muttered, sinking deeper into the couch.

"Hey, you guys," Mr. Cessna said, trying to buoy his

children's spirits. "What kind of attitude is this? Kidco may be down, but there's no reason for it to be out."

"We've been kayoed by the courts," Bette said glumly.

"Nipped in the butt," NeNe whimpered.

"That's bud, honey," Mrs. Cessna corrected, "and you haven't been nipped there at all. Like your father said, there's no reason why you kids can't rebound from this. Sure, you may have to pay a stiff fine, but from now on you'll be protected! You'll have the State off your back."

"Mom," Dickie said, staring remorsefully at the sales graph on the wall. "We didn't make all that money just to lose it."

"We know that, son," Mr. Cessna cut in. "It's a tough break, but when the going gets tough..."

"Yeah, yeah, the tough get going," Dickie groused. "I just don't feel that tough anymore, that's all...."

NeNe happened to glance up and see the time. Dragging herself from the couch, she went over and flicked on the portable television set.

"Hey, NeNe, what's the big idea?" June complained.

"It's after seven," NeNe said as she changed the station.

"NeNe," Bette chided, "do you have to watch *The People's Court tonight*?"

"The network news is on," NeNe defended herself. "I just wanted to see if they're showing our interview...."

As the image on the screen flickered into focus, the others watched doubtfully. NeNe's hunch was proven correct, however, for they all instantly recognized the courtyard in the background behind a reporter who was describing the trial that had taken place earlier.

"The courtyard is vacant now, as is the courtroom itself," the reporter droned, staring out at his unseen audience, "but the trial that has taken place here the past few days remains fresh in the minds of all those who have witnessed any part of the proceedings. It has been, from the start, a David and Goliath story, pitting a handful of enterprising children against the structured bureaucracy of one of the largest states in the nation. Those children, however, claim they're making a stand on behalf of their countless peers throughout the country. As Kidco President Dickie Cessna told reporters earlier today..."

At this point, the broadcast switched to a taped excerpt,

showing Dickie, dressed in his attorney outfit, fielding questions from a bevy of reporters crowding around the courtyard steps. On the screen, a spirited, feisty Dickie was saying, "People are always telling kids to get off their butts and do some work. Well, we did and we got busted for it! And if we let 'em do it to us, the paperboys'll be next!"

Watching himself, Dickie grimaced slightly. "Boy that sure seems like a long time ago."

"That was just this morning," his mother reminded him. "Take a good look at yourself up there on the screen, then take a look at yourself now . . . you, too, girls!"

On the screen, the Cessna girls were standing proudly behind their brother, looking ready to take on the whole world. The image was in striking contrast to the downhearted appearance of the children now. One of the reporters asked them, "So you feel you're fighting for other children as well as yourselves?"

"That's right!" Dickie said perkily on television. "We got a lot of letters when we went on TV before, and we know a lot more kids feel just like we do. We only wish they could all come here to San Diego to show these pencil pushers they can't push us kids around . . . !"

Up in the loft, Dickie made a face as he went over to the television set and turned it off, muttering, "How disgusting! Boy, was I full of it. . . ."

"Dickie . . ."

Before his mother could say anything more, Dickie cut her off, heading for the ladder, "I'm real tired. I didn't get much sleep last night, so I'm going to crash early. 'Night."

Mr. and Mrs. Cessna looked at one another, not sure what to do. They decided to leave him alone and called out together, "Good night, Dickie." Mr. Cessna added, "Things'll look better in the morning, son."

"I'm pretty sleepy, too," Bette yawned, getting up from the couch.

"Me, too," NeNe said, joining her two sisters as they headed for the ladder. Mr. and Mrs. Cessna remained up in the loft, however, and as soon as their children were gone from sight, Mr. Cessna quickly flicked the television set back on so that they could catch the last of the news segment on their children's legal entanglements.

"I'm about ready to cry myself," Mrs. Cessna admitted

as she waited for the picture to materialize on the screen. "They've worked so hard to have it end up turning out so badly."

"Who knows?" Mr. Cessna said, trying to cling to his hopes in the face of the prevailing pessimism. "They managed to pull out a miracle to beat the tax men. Maybe there'll be another one."

"I don't know where it would come from," Mrs. Cessna said, unaware that, at the very same moment, there were millions of television sets throughout the land tuned into the same news program, with even more millions of children watching and listening to the tenacious foursome of Kidco raising a rallying cry to the youth of America. With that many million ears, it seemed highly unlikely that *any* call would go unheard. . . .

Thirty-nine

As they took their seats at the defense table for the last time, the Cessna children were still in the throes of misery. None of them had been able to sleep well, and they had spent much of the night huddled together in Dickie's room, exchanging stories about their exploits of the past months for Kidco, telling them in the way relatives talk about the dearly departed at a funeral wake. This morning they were feeling both grief and bitterness, and the presence of an overflowing gallery filled with peer supporters was not even sufficient enough to bolster them with encouragement. Behind them, Mr. and Mrs. Cessna stood in the first row, concerned parents to the end. When Mrs. Cessna saw the bailiff reaching for the gavel to begin the day's business, she coughed to get the attention of the Defendants.

"Children," she said as she clasped her husband's hand for support, "I just want all four of you to know that these last couple days, and all the months preceding it, you've made your father and I the proudest parents in the world."

"Yeah, and they've made us the four poorest kids," Dickie said dismally.

"Thanks, Mom," June said. She smiled bravely at her father and blew Frank a kiss, then joined her brother and sisters in turning around to face the bench as the bailiff pounded the gavel for silence.

"All rise!"

Judge Willoughby entered the courtroom to his usual introduction, then quickly sat down and told the gallery before him to do the same. Plunging right into matters, he said, "It has been brought to the court's attention that the Defendants wish to change their pleas on the remaining charges."

This came as a surprise to most of the spectators, and Judge Willoughby had to resort to his gavel to keep their reaction from getting out of hand. Out in the gallery, only Orville Peterjohn seemed pleased with the unexpected change of events. His son was nowhere to be seen.

"Before those pleas are entered," Judge Willoughby went on, "I wish to commend the Department of Food and Agriculture, for its intention to make special allowances that will enable Kidco to resume its gopher control program."

The judge was expecting the chorus of cheers that greeted this announcement, and he began pounding away the moment he stopped talking. Still, it was a good fifteen seconds before the courtroom was quiet enough for him to resume.

"However, this court must still rule on the conduct of Kidco's officers in the past. And so, albeit with great sympathy, I will hear their new pleas to charges of violating the Food and Agricultural Code of the State of California."

The courtroom fell more silent than it had been when Judge Willoughby had begun his remarks. He nodded to the clerk, who, in turn, faced the Cessna children and said, "The Defendants will rise."

One by one, Dickie, Bette, NeNe, and June got up from their chairs, pictures of abject remorse, their heads hanging low, awaiting the worst.

"June Cessna," the clerk asked. "How do you plead?"

"Guilty," June whispered hoarsely.

There were a few moans and boos from the gallery. Pounding his gavel, Judge Willoughby admonished, "If I have to use this once more, I'll have to have the courtroom cleared. Don't force my hand."

With order swiftly restored, the clerk went on, "Bette Cessna, how do you plead?"

"Guilty," Bette said. Behind her, Mrs. Cessna began to weep, squeezing her husband's hand tighter. He looked as if he were about to cry as well.

"Richard Cessna, Junior, how do you plead?"

Dickie closed his eyes and mumbled, "Guilty."

"Jeannine Cessna, how do you plead?"

NeNe hesitated, unable to bring herself to speak until Dickie prodded her with his elbow.

"Guilty," she sniffed, "but it stinks!"

The silence in the courtroom mirrored the gloom at the defense table. Even Orville Peterjohn was having trouble expressing joy in the face of the circumstances. He grinned, but it wasn't the grin of a totally contented man. He looked more like someone who'd gone on a spending spree and had just received the bill for his extravagance.

"The court accepts these pleas," Judge Willoughby said, "and, in accordance with the laws of the State of California, fines the Defendants the sum of fifty dollars for each violation. . . ."

There were a few formalities to be seen to, but for all practical purposes the trial was over. Judge Willoughby concluded his remarks, then excused himself from the bench, giving the Defendants one last, sorrowful look before retiring to his chambers, followed closely by his campaign manager. The Cessna children joined their parents, who hugged them tightly, then helped lead them from the courtroom and into the lobby, which proved to be even more crowded than the gallery. Photographers, reporters, and fans all beseiged the Cessnas, speaking in unison, trying to get a piece of their time, if not a piece of the kids themselves. The atmosphere was almost frantic.

"Please!" Mr. Cessna shouted, trying to part the waves of people around them. "This has been a rough time for the kids. They need some time alone. . . ."

"We could use some money, too," Dickie added drearily.

A group of policemen appeared at the fringe of the crowd, threading their way through the masses. They managed to take up positions around the Cessna family just as they were approaching the main doors leading to the outside courtyard.

"Mr. Cessna," one of the officers called out, "We'd appreciate you not going out there. It could start a riot."

"What? Are you kidding?" Mr. Cessna said.

"Please, take my word," the officer told him.

Stopping just short of the doors, the family began to hear a faint, but growing, roar sounding outside the building. It seemed as if there was a cheering section out there, reciting the same two syllables over and over, louder with each repetition.

"What are they shouting?" Mrs. Cessna asked worriedly.

Straining to hear above the competing sounds inside the lobby, the four children were finally able to make out the words, and an incredible transformation began to overtake them. The dying spark of their old spunk was fanned into a full-blown flame, and Dickie was the first to perk up to the point where he was able to cry out excitedly, "What are they shouting?!! Mom, it's clear as day!"

In unison, the four children broke away from their parents and slipped past the policemen before they had a chance to react.

"Hey, don't!" one of the officers shouted futilely.

Throwing open the main doors, the four junior executives stepped outside to face a gathering of supporters that defied their wildest expectations. There were thousands of children, clotting the entire courtyard and spilling out into the road, blocking traffic. Directly across from the courtyard was a large, multistory parking structure, and that too was filled with children, all of them waving their hands and shouting at the tops of their lungs. Makeshift banners hung from the parking structure, identifying Kidco Fan Club Chapters from all over the Southwest. San Diego, Escondido, El Cajon, Yuma, Indio, Brawley, Blythe, Los Angeles, Palm Springs. And they were all shouting the same thing.

"Kidco! *Kidco!* KIDCO! *KIDCO!*"

Once Dickie had led his sisters into view of the entire assembly, the chant gave way to a rousing, deafening ovation. The cry grew increasingly louder, showing no signs of dissipating. Mr. and Mrs. Cessna emerged from the courthouse and joined their children, overwhelmed by the display of support.

"Well, I'll be . . ." Mr. Cessna said in awe.

Down near the street, Orville Peterjohn was battling his way through the throng, trying to make his way to his car. He was clearly flustered by the underaged crowd, which was too busy watching the Cessnas to bother getting out of his way.

"You brats are blocking the parking lot!" he railed uselessly. When he spotted his son among the other children, he turned red with rage and bellowed, "Harvey! I told you I didn't want you here today!"

There were a couple dozen other children between Harvey and his father, and the buffer gave him enough nerve to shout back, "I didn't want to be the only kid in school not here!"

"Ahhhhhhhh, you worthless little twerp!" Orville raved, throwing up his hands in despair.

As the Cessna family headed down the steps, now flanked by the police escort, two familiar faces forged their way through the crowd toward them. Skip Russo, trusty Louisville Slugger in hand, was clearing the way for Neil Brody, who was holding a large cardboard box close to his chest. One of the officers was about to send them on their way when Dickie reached out, restraining him as he shouted, "Hey! Those two are with us!"

The officer let Skip and Neil through the human barricade as they all paused at the bottom of the steps. Neil wearily dropped the box at Dickie's feet, then slumped to the steps, looking as if he'd just gotten back from the war front. Bette was quick to crouch down beside him.

"Neil!" she asked him. "What happened?"

"I was taking orders for T-shirts," Neil explained between breaths, gesturing to the box. Bette brought it over and Neil stuck his spindly hand in, coming up with a handful of paper scraps, gum wrappers, napkins, cards—all bearing names and addresses. Inside the box were more of the same.

"Jeez!" Dickie cried out, dumbfounded by the sight. "How many did you get, Neil?"

"How many kids are here?" Neil asked, cracking a grin. "At twenty percent commission, I'm going to be able to start up my own newspaper!"

"Oh, Neil, how wonderful!" Bette said, giving the beleaguered reporter a hug. Neil blushed the color of cranberries.

Dickie stood on his tiptoes, trying to gauge the size of

the multitude crowding the area around the courthouse. He had no way of being sure. He only knew that, at five dollars a T-shirt, Kidco had just found itself with a new market that stood a chance of rivaling their manure-selling and gopher-killing businesses combined.

The officer in charge of the police force dealing with the demonstration made his way over to the Cessna clan, carrying a bullhorn, which he promptly handed to Dickie, telling him, "These folks aren't going to disperse peacefully until you say something to them."

"Okay," Dickie said eagerly. Surrounded by his family and the handful of policemen, he climbed back up to the top step and waved his hands, trying to calm the crowd to the point where they would be able to hear him. Then, hoisting the bullhorn, he called out, "Hello, everybody!"

"HELLO!" came the thunderous reply from the legions before him. Mixed in were a wide range of other cheers, most noticeably the voices of young girls calling Dickie by name.

"My sisters and me want to thank you all for showing up today," Dickie ad-libbed. "And we want to tell you that you just helped us make enough dough to pay our fine . . . *and* maybe still have enough to give rebates on the T-shirts!"

Again the ovation resounded, filling the afternoon. Heaps of confetti found their way into the air and were carried by the breeze blowing through town. Goaded on by the show of support, Dickie beamed at his parents and sisters, then exhorted through the bullhorn, "Maybe now these bozos'll pick on someone their own size!"

As the crowd began lapsing back into its chant of 'Kidco! KIDCO!', the Cessnas crowded together, basking in the adulation. From the brink of defeat, they'd found themselves raised not only back to their feet, but back to a position of financial well-being. Swept up by his own euphoria, Dickie found himself already concocting a new scheme. He sized up the multitude, then extricated himself from his sisters and once again addressed his following.

"I also want to take this opportunity to announce plans for a *new* Kidco T-shirt! This one will have not only our name, but also a picture of the company president! To order—"

June and Bette simultaneously reached over and grabbed the bullhorn, pulling it away from their brother.

"What about *our* pictures!?" Bette demanded angrily.

"Hey!" Dickie said, thinking fast, "Those are the next three in the series. . . ."

"I wanna be on the first one!" NeNe squealed, poking Dickie with an insistent forefinger.

"Sorry, I veto that suggestion," Dickie countered glibly.

"What?" all three sisters shouted at once.

As the foursome continued to argue, behind them their parents looked at one another, smiling gratefully. No one was going to say that success had changed their children. . . .